Holiday High

James Arthur

Books to Hook
PUBLISHING

Holiday High

First Edition: September 2023

ISBN 978-1-962071-30-7 (ebook)
ISBN 978-1-962071-29-1 (paperback)

Published by Books to Hook Publishing, LLC.
www.BooksToHook.com

For Christiana and Noelle. You are my everything.

CONTENTS

CHAPTER ONE

I don't know why I have to go to Holiday High. I was perfectly fine attending my own high school. Yes, it was big, but that's what I loved about it. Being invisible is what I loved.

Three thousand students—my old school had three thousand glorious students for me to hide among. But not now. Now, I have to go to Holiday High, with a student body of, maybe, 20?

Arbor Day is doing just fine. Sure, it's not the biggest holiday. It's not Christmas, nor Valentine's Day. It isn't even April Fool's Day. But it's fine. Those who celebrate it are the most loyal and dedicated of any holiday celebrators. There is no hype. No need for pop culture icons. No crazy tree mascot. They actually want to celebrate. They care, and that's what I care about. I don't need Holiday High.

But here I stand, a girl who is literally on the steps of the school, trying to will herself to go in. My goodness, I've become a cliché—the new girl who is afraid of the first day of school! How pathetic. My parents were so thrilled when the letter came:

Dear Mr. and Mrs. Day, Congratulations! Your holiday has been deemed worthy of acceptance in the elite school for holiday preparation, Holiday High. Go Spirit!

Yes.

They are the Fighting Holiday Spirit. How awful. It has been decades since Arbor Day has been recognized as big enough to attend Holiday High. My father never got to go. His father never got to go. You have to go back three generations to find the last time Arbor Day got to attend. How lucky am I?

Thus, I stand in front of this immaculate brick building with the flags of the holidays proudly waving from poles atop the roof. It has nice trees and a nice lawn. This fancy aura makes me want to vomit! Do I really have to live here for eight months? Does no one else see the irony that Flag Day has a flag waving? I see the irony. But then again, I always do. No way am I going to be invisible here.

"Just try and make the best of it, Arbor," my dad pleaded with me. It's what must have been the one-hundredth fight we had on the subject. Still, it was a week out at this point, and I wasn't exactly coming around to the idea. "This is a huge honor. Something our family has been trying to attain for the longest time." Dad's protestations fell on deaf ears. "I know it's not what you would have chosen, but try your best."

"My dear, it's important to maintain connections with others," Mother reminded. "Make some friends. Talk to people. You can be very charming when you give it an effort." "So basically, don't be me?" I mutter. "Be happy. Be excited! Be the best Arbor Day I can be!"

"That sarcasm isn't going to help you at all. Try dialing that down some," Dad added. "Make sure people know how smart you are and how thoughtful you are before you resort to sarcasm. The world famous Arbor sarcasm certainly won't help you at the Confirmation."

The Confirmation. How I already dread that word. Seven months away, and I hate it already. The Confirmation is the time each year when the student of each holiday presents to the faculty the importance and plans for their particular holiday. It's just a formality for "The Majors," like Christmas, New Year's Eve, and Halloween. For others, "The Minors," it can be a make-or-break time.

If your holiday is losing traction in America, you can be dismissed from Holiday High. For me, this is the most important Confirmation I will have. The outcome will determine whether I will have a second year, and if so, it will supposedly be easier to maintain my Confirmed Status. But I cannot shake the dreaded mindset that I don't want to be here.

I don't want to be part of this world. I don't want to be "confirmed." All I ever wanted to do was what my parents do-- travel the country teaching the importance of Arbor Day. They speak at schools, church groups, and to college students in malls, stores, parks, and basically anywhere else where people will listen. I want to continue my weekend lessons where I teach students the importance of our holiday at the national park near where we live. I don't want the prestige of being a confirmed holiday even if it means that more trees are planted, and more people will recognize and support our holiday. I don't know why I have to go to Holiday High.

Eight steps. Eight steps to the top. Eight steps to the top, to the doors. Eight steps to the top, to the doors, and inside. That's all it takes to enter a world that I've only been told about. To be honest, I never thought I would even have to be in this situation. My legs are cement. There is no way I'm going to make it up these eight steps. I need to find a way to motivate my way to the top, to the doors, and to go inside. I can't help but wonder if this is all pointless.

"Just take it one step at a time," I tell myself out loud. With each step, I need to find something positive to get myself moving. I chuckle and realize that self-motivation is going to be a big part of my life now. I groan and realize that it does not seem possible to find anything positive in all of this.

Step one. I miraculously lift my right foot off the ground and up. I imagine this is what an elephant feels like lifting its feet. I plant it on the first step.

"This is a good thing. It's a chance for more people to recognize the greatness of Arbor Day." The left foot follows. Step one done.

Step two. Elephant foot starts up again. "More trees will be planted. If that's the end game to all this; then, it matters." Step two conquered.

"Maybe I will find a true friend." "My parents are proud of me."

"If anything I can sabotage all the other holidays." Steps three, four, and five down. "Aren't new experiences supposed to be character building?" "No boys liked me at City High. Maybe a boy will like me here."

Now, step seven is a reach. Not many boys have proven to handle my obvious, snarky, unique brand of communication. It's pretty common that when I think I'm hilarious others think I'm just weird. I handle this by just not talking to boys. It has proven to be a very effective way to not get hurt or to get wrapped up in the frivolous drama that comes with giving the opposite sex an inch into your world.

So, step eight is here. It's not too late to back out. Descending down the steps will go faster than moving up them. It would be easy to come up with eight reasons to leave. But is there really a good enough reason that will give me the strength to make this last big step?

"I hate this establishment. I hate what it stands for. I hate how it makes the decision on who is 'deemed worthy.' I'm going to go in there and show them that all holidays are worthy. All holidays are not here to simply let them control us into being what they want us to be. I'm Arbor Day. I deem myself worthy. I really need a nap." With that, I feel my feet practically move themselves up the last hurdle. Step eight down. In your face, Holiday High!

Now at the top, I paused to ponder the victory that's making it to the top. I imagine my parents being so happy--cheering me on. It's a far cry from the last conversation we had at the airport. "I don't want to hear this again," Dad said. "I'm just done arguing with you. I'm drained. You are an amazing young lady, and Holiday High is lucky to have you. You can take our holiday and make it the best it has ever been if you would simply stop fighting. The Holiday Council will not control your life. Only you control you. Trust me, I know."

"What your father is trying to say, Arbor, is just be careful," Mom offers, shooting my father a stern look. "You are my girl, Arbor."

"Mom, please don't cry. Crying may just make me run. You do know that running through an airport like a madwoman is frowned upon, right?"

"I'm not going to cry, dear. Just please stop with the bitterness. While you're at it, you can let the anger go too. Use it. Use it to show them what the Days are all about. Show them the importance of our holiday. Let 'em have it."

"Mushy stuff?" My Dad says, waiting for our version of "I love you." I never like the words. It's so overused. So I simply say "mushy stuff" when I can't decide how to express my love for someone.

"Always mushy stuff to you both," I say gently, letting them hug me. Only because I know hugs make them happy. Staring at these gigantic glass doors with the HH logo etched in each pane. Their words are running through my mind like an old record on skip. "Use it. Use it. Use it." Can I really do this? Open the doors and enter into this world? "Use it," I say to myself. I reached for the doors and opened them.

CHAPTER TWO

W ell, I will say this about Holiday High: it smells really good. It's like they took all the smells of all the holidays and mixed them into one scent. Imagine peppermint, fireworks, pumpkin, and pine all mixed together; you would think it would be totally disgusting, but here, it works. As much as I hate to admit it, but the first thing I think is, "This smells very nice." But I need to stop it. That's how they get you. They make it feel like home, and then, they sneak in and get you. No way! Good smell or not, I won't let them suck me in.

I take in my surroundings. I'm in some sort of foyer. A giant throw rug is spread across the floor. Again, the HH logo is prominently featured in the center, this time in the school colors of red, green, and white. It sits in the middle, surrounded by chairs and couches that just call me for a nap. There is the biggest brick fireplace that you can imagine. Despite my not wanting to be here, I can't help but long for a winter day to sit near a fire burning.

"Stop liking this place!" I chastise myself. Looking down one way, I see a wooden hall, and down the other it's the same. Before you hit the hallways, there are big staircases leading up to the second and third floors.

My timing seems to be perfect as the bell rings as soon as I stop looking around. I only have my backpack with me, as all my other stuff was shipped a week ago, and it's supposed to be waiting for me in my room. Right now, I just feel like a lost girl looking up in the sky for her balloon that has floated away. I wish I could float away. But superpowers aren't real. But that would be cool, though. A private school for teens with superpowers, now, that would be something.

I really should have come a day earlier so I could have at least known where to go. But in my stubbornness, I wanted to stay in my normal life as long as I could. As I'm looking around admiring the tall windows (man, they really, really like this HH logo), I hear shoes clacking toward me and look to see who is headed my way. Coming towards me from one of the hallways is a tall slender man. He is dressed in a dark blue suit, with a dark blue tie, and a dark blue shirt. When he glides up to me, I notice he has pale white skin and the whitest hair I've ever seen, which is slicked back over the crown of his head. Also, he has a really pointy nose. Like a woodpecker, I think. I have to stifle a laugh.

This winsome figure makes his way closer to me. As he approaches, I start to feel a cold chill in the air. Not just any chill, it's like your bones hurt, and your lower back is killing you kind of chill. He stops just short of knocking into me. That's when I first notice his eyes—ice cold blue. Glacier blue. Being this close, the chill is unbearable. Who is this guy?

"Hmmmmm," he says, looking me up and down with his frostbite eyes. "Long brown hair, tall and slender. You have long arms, long legs, and those green eyes. You must be Arbor Day." He says this while calmly walking around me in a slowly calculated circle. The combination of the chill and his eyes is enough to make me forget all about any homey smells.

"Yes," I say tentatively. Is that really my voice right now? Like a weak orphan asking for more. "I'm Arbor... um...Arbor Day. I'm supposed to be going to school here now." Chill Man stops right in front of me. The cold seems to grow greater as he starts at the top of my head, slowly looking me down to my feet and back up again a second time.

"You will come with me right now." He speaks in a calm, cold way. He turns and starts toward the stairway on the left side. I stay frozen. I'm too cold to actually calculate what I'm supposed to be doing. As he gets to the first step, he doesn't even turn towards me. "You will follow me right now," he repeats. Something stirs in me and my feet start to unfreeze, and I move forward.

Chill Man slowly starts up the stairs, and I follow. I half expect the stairs to be covered in ice where his footfalls have landed on the carpet and for me to fall to my death after slipping on one of the deadly impressions. Actually, that may be for the best. I'm following an odd stranger upstairs to who knows where. When exactly did I outgrow stranger danger? I find my voice and speak up.

"Um, who are you?" I stammer as we make it to the top of the staircase. I'm expecting to stop, but we keep going.

"I'm Jack Frost, Vice Principal of Holiday High," he says in that cold, slow way. A way that I imagine molasses would speak if it were alive. "You will not ask any more questions until we arrive."

"Arrive where?" I blurt out.

"YOU will not ask any more questions," he snaps, turning sharply around and staring me right in the eyes. The cold chill rises through me like a flash freeze, and I feel like I'm ice. "You will learn right now that I'm one who you will respect here. You will learn to answer me and do what I say without question. You will learn that not everyone is excited about you being here."

The words prick at me like millions of pieces of small hail. A cold sweat breaks out all over my body. I oddly start to worry that I might catch a cold even though it's still early September and seasonably warm outside.

"Do you understand me now, Day?" The way he says my last name sparks anger inside me. I feel some warmth coming back through the chill. I don't like being talked down to. People thinking they are better than me without even knowing me is something I do not tolerate.

"I understand, Frost," I say through cold, angry teeth.

Standing up straight, Frost breathes an exasperated sigh. "You will continue to follow me now in silence." He turns back around, and we commence up the stairs. Thankful for the movement, I start to feel my arms and legs thaw out. We keep rising until we reach the top of the third set of stairs. There, we take a left, and he leads me down yet another hallway. Wooden walls and floors are broken up by doors on either side. Each door has a golden nameplate emblazoned with the name of a holiday— Valentine's Day, April Fool's' Day, Memorial Day, and the list goes on. I start to gather we must be in the female wing of the dormitories.

"You will reside here in this room," Frost says, stopping. I look to the right and left of me. I'm sandwiched between two other rooms. "Groundhog's Day," reads one, and "Columbus Day," says the other. I find it interesting that I'm going to be stuck between a person who wants to see their shadow and another who supposedly discovered America.

"You will go inside. You will find your uniform and put it on. You will wait until you hear the next bell ring dismissing the other students from the morning assembly. You will then make your way back downstairs, where you will be met by me, and I will take you to meet the Principal. You will not ask me any questions now." And with that, Frost turned and slowly made his way back down the hall. I'm so thankful that the cold went with him.

I stand there for a second, letting myself thaw out, and I admire the gold plate on my door.

Arbor Day is engraved in a fancy script. The marker is about a foot long and a foot wide, and it looks to be pure gold. In each corner, there is the HH logo is carved into to it. It's then that it truly hits me; I live here. My true home may have been left behind yesterday as I flew here, but this, at least for eight long months, is going to be my home.

I reached for the handle and stepped inside. I'm instantly mad. Of course, it would be wonderful. In one corner, there is a large wooden wardrobe of beautiful wood. A desk sits next to it. On the desk is a set of red pens and green pens. There are four different notebooks, all of the different shades of red and green. Designed on the front of each one is one word: English, Math, Science, and History.

The far wall holds a dresser and a full-length mirror. Small chandeliers run along the ceiling, not giving off much light as individuals, but together they join to form a light that isn't too bright but not too soft, like sunlight filtering through a forest canopy. Sitting between the bed and the wardrobe is an oversized chair that sits underneath the only window in the room. Then, I really notice the bed. Even from the doorway, I can tell it's beyond comfortable. It has four posts, each carved into the design of a tree. The bed sits up so high that I'm given two small steps on which to climb up into it. Sitting beside the steps is my trunk. I eagerly head to it, desperate to open it up and get something from home. I'm about to bend down to open it when I notice something lying on the bed —my uniform.

"Of course it looks great," I sigh to myself. The uniform consists of a nice pair of dark red slacks that feel like heaven, a starched white, long-sleeved shirt, a red and green sweater vest, dark green socks, and black shoes. I'm also given a green and red hair ribbon, which I assume is for accessorizing my hair. I get a sick feeling again as I realize that this is exactly the type of uniform that I would have selected. I hate myself for liking it.

I slowly put on the uniform, taking my time to marvel at how amazing it feels and how perfect it fits. I take the green ribbon, and instead of using it for my hair, I tie it around my neck so it looks like my neck is the present. Plus, I hope it helps with the chill that seems to come with Frost. After I'm finished, I gather up the four notebooks, thinking I may need them, eventually. Stuffing them in my backpack, I add the pens. I sit down in the chair.

Tempted to take a nap, I marvel at the fact that I'm so exhausted, and it's not even 9 A.M. yet. My eyes start to feel heavy when a loud ringing penetrates through my tiredness. I sigh and stand. I have no desire to face Frost again, but I'm also fearful that if I linger, I will feel that cold again. I take one final glance around, hoping that this time I hate what I see. But no, all I feel is that I can't wait to come back and sleep. I shake out my hands, throw on my pack, and open the door.

CHAPTER THREE

I make my way back down the way Frost brought me. As I get closer to the lower level, I hear laughter and talking coming from the foyer. Suddenly, I become slow. Not only do I not want to face Frost, but I definitely don't want to face my new class-mates. For now, I'm still invisible. I'm sure they have heard that a new Minor holiday has been deemed worthy to attend Holiday High, but they have yet to meet me or see me. I continue down slowly, lingering long enough until I don't hear any more noise. I descend take the second flight and stop at the landing top.

I look down and see Frost waiting there. I can already feel the chill. I make my way down, conscious that he's watching every step. When I get to the bottom, I stand meekly waiting to be told what to do. You know, since I'm not allowed to ask him questions at all. Frost takes a long look at me and seems to be repulsed at the way I look.

"You will dress like this every day you attend this school. You may change little things, but overall, I'm surprised that you have been able to present yourself in such a fine manner. You will now follow me," Frost orders as he turns towards the same hallway where he first appeared earlier this morning. I dutifully follow him.

I released the breath I didn't even know I was holding, and it mists in the chill air, trailing my guide.

This hallway is very similar to the residence hallway. It has the same wooden floors, and its walls are also interrupted by doors. These doors, however, have windows in them. I sneak a peak in one and see it's cluttered with every piece of sports equipment you can imagine. Right in the middle is a desk with all types of film tapes piled everywhere. Coach Bunyan, it reads in black script on the glass.

"You will stop looking at what you should not be bothered with," Frost hollers back at me, and I pick up my step. We make our way down the hall, with the doors getting fewer and fewer. I realize that means the offices must be getting bigger. I know we're on our way to the Principal. I begin to wonder what type of person runs this school. If Frost is any inclination, then the top person has to be even more of a piece of work. I don't know if I can handle two such obtuse figures running my life. I'm in such deep thought I barely notice Frost stopping right in front of me.

"This is the Principal's office," He informs. "You will never go in here unless requested.

You will sit there quietly and speak only when spoken to. You will say nothing and will do nothing that will make me look bad in her eyes. You need to understand that I'm to be respected at all times." Her? A female principal? I don't know if I'm to be excited or scared. I can't imagine a woman who can control Frost, so maybe she's just as bad or worse. Frost knocks on the door and opens it.

"Principal Fairy, I have Arbor Day to see you." What voice is that? Frost suddenly changes it all up. Lighter tone, faster pace, what a sneaky devil. He cannot be trusted. Frost enters, and I follow. If Frost is the cold, icy side of life then Principal Fairy is his opposite. I'm instantly engulfed in warmth. Standing up to greet me is the tallest woman I've ever seen. She has long strawberry-blonde hair and is dressed in a very stylish green dress. The dress isn't causal but also not fancy. It comes respectfully down to her knee and fits snugly around her top. On one wrist she has a red watch and the other a red bracelet. I actually think there is a light glowing behind her.

"Arbor Day, it's so nice to finally meet you," she says, gleaming. "Everyone here is so excited that you have joined us here at Holiday High. Aren't we, Frost?" She looks up at him with an eager expression that clearly invites him to agree with her. "We are so happy to have her here," Frost sings songs again in that all too fake voice.

"Please sit down, Arbor. We have much to talk about."

I'm directed to a chair directly across from her. There is another chair by me, and I brace myself for Frost to make himself at home, too. He does not, however, move; he continues to stand by the door he led us in. I wonder if his legs are so cold that they would break if he bends them to sit down.

The office I'm in is full but cozy. It's painted a nice shade of light red, not quite pink. The walls are covered with paintings that draw you in. There seems to be one to represent each of the holidays. I see a ship sailing, a party on the streets of New Orleans, and brilliant fireworks so real that you can almost hear the bang-pop of their explosions. I laugh as I see one of a bunny hopping around with a basket.

"Ah yes, my paintings," Principal Fairy gestures to the walls. "When a holiday reaches confirmed status, I add it my wall. As you see, there isn't a painting reflecting your holiday, but that's all going to change this year, isn't it?" She offers me the most sincere smile I've ever seen. So sincere it makes me uncomfortable. I didn't think it was possible for a person to be this caring.

"Arbor, I'm Principal Tooth Fairy, but all the students simply call me Fairy. This is going to be a wonderful year for you, my dear. It has been ages since Arbor Day has been in attendance here, and it's an event that's to be celebrated. From speaking with your parents, I understand you're a very bright young lady--even though you harbor some hesitations about coming this year."

"Hesitation" is an understatement. I sense that I'm going to be asked something hard and be expected to open up. That isn't my favorite thing. I hold my thoughts and feelings close.

Ironically, I often think of it like ice surrounding them. I'm sure Frost would love that. I'm sure his heart is surrounded by an iceberg if there is a heart in there. Stupid feelings!

"So, Arbor, what is this hesitation all about?" Fairy calmly asks me. My fists clench, and I stop breathing. Why does she have to be so nice?

"I...I wouldn't call it hesitation. That isn't the right word." I speak slowly, trying to think before I speak. My father would be so proud right now.

"Well then, Arbor, what would you call it?"

"Well, just plain old-fashioned, not wanting to come," I say. Instantly, I regret saying it. Why do I always have to be so blunt? Never mind, my father would be horrified, but Fairy starts to chuckle.

"Well then, Arbor, that's something totally different." Fairy sits up straight and folds her hands on the desk. She takes a moment and just looks at me. Unlike earlier when Frost, the Creeper, was checking me out, this does not make me nervous. I feel warmth come over me, and again, I swear she's glowing.

"Arbor, listen to me. No one here is out to hurt you. No one here is out to change you. In fact, Holiday High solely exists to make you the best person and, therefore, the best holiday you can be. We are going to open a world to you that's wonderful. There is no need for hesitation about being here. You were chosen by the Holiday Council to be deemed worthy. I'm the head of that council, and I guarantee that your success is all we seek here."

"Well put, Principal Fairy," chimes in Frost. My stomach turns again at the sound of that repulsive voice of his. At the same time, I have the sensation of warmth on my front and cold on my back. Like a battle of what I'm truly doing here is starting to form in my presence.

"The teachers here are the best in their fields," Fairy continues. "They will challenge you. I'm not going to lie to you about that. But in that challenge, I feel you will start to grow and blossom. Pun intended."

"Thank you," I say as calmly as I can. "I promised my parents that I would try hard." I don't know exactly how much more I'm supposed to say or open up. But the fact that Fairy was encouraged by my honesty earlier helped me decide to try that route again.

"This is very hard for me. I like to blend in, to be invisible. I felt that our holiday was doing fine," I say, trying hard to fight the rage inside me. "I don't need you to deem me worthy. Every tree that's planted in April deems me and my family worthy." I slow my breath. I really don't want to get so upset right here, right now, and especially in front of Frost.

"Yes, Arbor, I believe you're worthy. Your holiday is one of the oldest and more traditional in our country." Fairy's chest starts to rise and the glow seems to get brighter. "But that's the whole point of you being here. This is your chance to take your holiday and make it bigger than it has ever been. Let us here at Holiday High help you do that. Won't you?"

I glance at the ceiling and try hard to think of the right thing to say. I want it to be something that will be both respectful and myself. With a short glance at the wall of paintings, I look back at Fairy. "I promised my parents I would try hard. And I want my holiday on that wall."

"Then let's make that happen. Frost, here is Arbor's schedule. Please escort her to her first class." Fairy rises and moves around to sit on the front of the desk and takes the time to look me over again. "Arbor, I think you're going to do great things here."

CHAPTER FOUR

We leave the office and its warmth to reenter the hallway. It may be my imagination, but the second the door closes, I'm engulfed in that cold chill again. I stand there waiting for Frost to reveal our next step.

"You did moderately well," Frost says, reverting back to his normal speech pattern. "You will now follow me as we make our way to..." He pauses to check my schedule.... "English."

He proclaims as he passes the schedule to my hands. I look at the green paper, reading the schedule for my new life. While my old school schedule could be quite confusing at times, in comparison, this is very simple to follow. I have the same schedule every day. "Track 4" is printed at the top. Below that, it reads: Morning Assembly, English, Math, Lunch, Science, P.E. MWF, Arts T/TH; History, and Mentoring. Mentoring? What is that?

I don't have time to reflect too much as Frost takes off down the hall. I reluctantly start to follow. This must be what a penguin feels like walking around Antarctica, trailing behind while walking through a tunnel of chilly wind. This time, I know better than to stop and look into the offices. Besides, all I'm thinking about is English—my first class. The invisibility is about to end.

Frost pulls up at the foot of the stairs. "You will never go to the third floor of this side of the school," he says, pointing up and not facing me. Again. "That's the boys' residence wing, and if you're caught there, you will face a meeting with the Holiday Council, and I will personally see that it leads to your expulsion."

"I understand," I answer. I've come to the conclusion that agreeing with Frost is the best route to take, even though every ounce of my soul screams to be snarky. Snarkiness, I assume, isn't high on Frost's list of favorite traits. So I will try my hardest to be a nice little agreeable Arbor, even if it costs me a bit of my soul each time. Frost turns and starts to point elsewhere.

"Down the other side of the first floor is the cafeteria, assembly hall, nurse's office, and the study lounge. You will not go into any of those unless you're supposed to. You may enter the study lounge at any hour. It's open at all times," Frost explains, moving his arms upwards. "You will find that all classrooms are located on the second floor. You know where the girls' residence wing is. You will report any male student that you see in the female residence wing to me. Let's move on."

With that, we start to climb. I have never experienced walking to my impending doom. Not much of that happens in your first fifteen years of life, but I can't imagine it can feel much different than this. We reach the top and turn right. Again, I'm greeted by wooden floors and walls. Stopping at the first door on the left, I see the word "English" on the window. Before I can gather the courage to face my firing squad, Frost is already opening the door.

"Hello, class," says Frost. NOT in the sing-song voice this time. "Our, um, new class member is here. She's Track 4. You will make sure that she's taken care of and shown where to go. You will do this or answer to me."

With that, he turns and leaves. Really? Just leave me standing here? I watch Frost depart, and I take a deep breath. Not too late to run, I think to myself. I step in.

"Hello!" exclaims a lady rushing towards me. "You must be Arbor! We are so excited you're here."

I'm engulfed in a giant hug, and I'm hit with a blast of perfume. It's such a rush of cinnamon and vanilla that I'm so overtaken I don't even have to think about how much I hate hugs. I practically fall back, my eyes stinging. I look up to see a huge, wide smile. The biggest smile I think I've ever seen. This teacher, at least I think she's the teacher, is a big lady to go with this big smile. She has short brown hair bobbing to her neck, which has glasses hanging around it. She's wearing a blouse with a long skirt that comes to the floor. Not surprisingly, her clothes are all red and green. I take a look and she seems to be looking at me like I'm the biggest cupcake in the world.

"I'm Ms. Grimm! Come on, give me another hug!" Grimm says, engulfing me again in a sweet bear hug. Wait, maybe this is what it feels like when a cupcake hugs you. I actually cough this time. It's so overwhelming.

"Oh, my dear, I'm so sorry. I'm a hugger," she says, clasping her hands together and giving me another mile-wide smile. "I'm just so excited you're here. My goodness, am I your first class? Please tell me I'm your very first class ever!"

"You are my very first class ever," I answer, my throat burning. "Well, not ever. But here, you are my very first class here."

"Oh my goodness, that's wonderful!" Before I know it, I'm engulfed again. This time, I'm picked up. Like picked up and raised off the floor. I just stay there limp, like a rag doll. I have no clue what to do right now.

I'm finally let go and allowed to take in my surroundings. The classroom is so different from any classroom that I've ever been in. The walls are dark green, and the floor is covered with a dark red carpet. Lamps are placed all around the room with red or green cloth over them, giving out a muted glow. A chalkboard takes up the wall in the front of the room. A big stool sits there as well. In the middle are six large bean bags. When I say big, I mean huge.

Bigger than some beds I've seen. Sitting in the bags are my first five classmates. I feel them staring at me. Well, because they are staring at me. Well, all but one who is actually asleep in the bag bed. "Class," proclaims Grimm, "this is Arbor Day. She's the new holiday here at school. Please welcome her. Show her how amazing Track 4 is."

Four students sit before me and the one is lying down...sleeping. There is a boy with slicked back blonde hair wearing a green suit with a red tie. Who wears a suit in high school? Two girls sitting close in the same bag giggling with each other. One is a girl who has dark brown skin. She wears a tight red top with a green skirt. It's obvious that not all the uniforms are the same. In her black, straight hair are two giant red hearts, which kind of make her look like a mouse. Sitting beside her is a pale, lanky girl with long strawberry-red hair. Many freckles live on her face. Many, many freckles. These two...ugh. The next two students look similar except that one, the girl, is all smiles and waving at me. Like I mentioned before, the boy is asleep. I'm trying to figure out exactly why he's sleeping when the suited boy rises.

"Greetings, Arbor Day, and welcome to Holiday High. Let me be the first to welcome you here and to Track 4. I'm President Day, but everyone calls me Pres." I'm not sure what to think right now after such a formal welcome.

"Does everyone have the last name Day?" I ask.

"Huh, not everyone," says Heart Mouse. "You see, when you're a major holiday like us," she says, motioning to Freckles, "we get to choose what last name we have. Day is for the Minors." Freckles just giggles.

"Now, that's Valentine," Pres says. "I'm sure she's happy you're here, too, in her own unique way."

"Nope," Valentine quips.

"But sadly, she's right," Pres continues. "You will find that many of the Minors do have the last name Day. Her bag buddy there is April. The other two...."

"I'm Spring!" interrupts the other girl, jumping up from her bag. "Welcome!" I don't know what to say to this hyper girl, and she, too, engulfs me in yet another hug. Is this place called Hugs High?

"This sleepyhead here is Fall. We are the Daylight Savings twins." Well, that explains why they look alike. Both seemed to be on the short side, and they both sported black hair and were obviously athletic. "Please excuse my brother. He takes the whole extra hour of sleep thing very seriously."

"I can't blame him. Sleep is the best," I say. More giggles come my way from Valentine and April. I really preferred the names Heart Mouse and Freckles.

"Arbor, please come, come. We have a special spot just for you," Grimm says, motioning me to the empty bag between Valentine and Pres. I gingerly sit down and am happy to find that it's more sturdy than I had imagined. Something then hits me.

"Grimm?" I question. "And you teach English?" I look up to see her getting settled on her stool.

"Why, yes!" she says with her smile stretching out the room. "My brothers are the world famous Grimm Brothers. But don't you worry. I'm not nearly as dark as they were. We only want to write lovely and happy things in here."

Well, that's a relief. The last thing I need is to tap into my dark side while here. I'm not sure how they would react to me writing about the school burning down. Even though I'm sure Frost would still be walking around the flames not feeling a thing. Grimm opens her teaching materials, and I dig out my red notebook that says English. I grab a red pen, because why not? "Why are you wearing pants?" Valentine asks me while looking at my legs. "Not very stylish, if you ask me."

"Really. Not stylish at all," April chimes in. "Because a long summer dress with smiley faces on it just screams runway?" I snap back. April did not like that. At all. I see her pale skin turn a dark crimson color and her eyes slit into the deathly stare of a psycho killer.

"Calm down, April," Valentine says calmly, putting her hand on April's shoulder. "She will learn her place soon enough." I was about to snap back at her that my place was not here anyway when Grimm clears her throat.

"Class, let's get started for the day. Spring, can you please wake Fall up?" She asks. Spring leans over to her brother and starts ruffling his hair.

"Fall," she says in a sweet, motherly voice. "It's time to wake up. We are in English class now." Fall gently opens his eyes and sits up. His dark black hair is all standing on end, and he seems confused as to where he is. He blinks around the room and then his eyes land on me.

"Who are you?" He asks. I think he's trying to figure if he's awake or dreaming. "That's Arbor. She's the new holiday," Spring responds. Fall continues to stare at me with a blank look.

"Ok," He says and opens his bag. The others grab their pens and notebooks, and we get settled.

"With today being the first day of the year, we're going to write an essay this week about what we want to accomplish for our holiday this year," Grimm explains, never once breaking her smile. "I want you to dream big. I want you to think of a place that has no limitations."

She starts motioning with her arms, red and green bracelets clanking with excitement. "Holiday High is the place where your holiday dreams can come true! Take those dreams and put them on paper. "

Now, I don't know what to think. I appreciate the fact that Grimm is beyond excited about the school year and her energy does make you want to do something. But right now, my goal for my holiday is for it to stay the same and for me to get out of here and back to life as usual. Grimm goes on to explain that the essay is due in four days on Friday. We will spend today working on brainstorming. I spend the rest of time trying to come up with some-thing, but at the end of class, all I've written is one sentence. "Get out of Holiday High."

I can't imagine how I'm going to get a whole essay out of one sentence or how this is going to be a goal for my holiday, but I don't have much time to think because the bell rings and I'm forced to pack up.

"Next, we have Math," Pres says as we're all standing and gath-ering our bags. "It's best not to be late. Old Man starts the second the bell rings and doesn't stop until the bell rings again."

"And don't even think about going to the bathroom," Spring offers, looping her arm in mine. "Come with me. I will make sure you're taken care of."

CHAPTER FIVE

W e make our way over to the other side of the second floor with Spring and Pres guiding me. I'm kind of at their mercy and don't really even get a chance to take a breath and process what I'm seeing. All the other holiday students are out changing classes as well. Spring and Pres take great pride in introducing me to everyone they see.

I don't remember anyone's name except Columbus, who I remember mainly because I'm her neighbor and she's a girl. For whatever reason, I thought Columbus would be a boy. She also stands out for her choice of uniform. A green tank top covered up by an unbuttoned red and green checkered flannel shirt. Tight green leggings and sneakers finish off her outfit. She has a red cap on backward with short brown hair sticking out. For some people this look would not work. Especially since LEGGINGS AREN'T PANTS! But for Columbus and her bronze skin, it works.

I'm still being paraded around when I notice that Valentine has stopped ahead of us to hug and cling to a tall, blonde, Norse god-looking student. April stands to the side like a too-small body-guard. "Who is that?" I ask as we move closer to the baseball jersey-wearing god. Also, BASEBALL JERSEYS AND JEANS DON'T GO TOGETHER!

"That's Santa, Valentine's boyfriend," Pres explains. "What he sees in her no one knows.

But he's part of the Big Four, and I think Valentine loves that. He isn't the brightest holiday, but he's a nice enough guy."

"Plus, he can throw a wicked curve ball," offers Fall, who is trailing along behind us. I don't have time to learn more as I enter into a classroom the complete opposite of Grimm's. This looks like a college classroom with white tables and green chairs. Up front is a whiteboard with a man standing there calmly. He isn't old, not young. He has balding white hair and wears glasses. He is dressed in a striped red and white shirt with green slacks. Oddly enough he has an actual pocket protector full of pens.

"Old Man," says Spring, "This is Arbor Day. She's the new holiday and part of Track 4." Old Man? Who is this Old Man? Oh, wait...I get it. He played one; he played one, knickknack. Irony.

"Welcome to Math," Old Man says in a bland voice. No emotion, no accent, nothing. I slide into a chair between Spring and Fall. I pull out my green notebook like the others and wait. I don't have to wait long. The bell rings and true to Pres' words, Old Man turns, opens his marker, and starts writing and talking. Also true, he does not stop until the end of class.

I feel like I have just sat through the most monotone lecture on earth. How we aren't all pulling a Fall and sleeping right now is beyond me. I'm dazed. I pull out my green schedule to look, but I'm stopped by Spring.

"Don't worry about this, dear. You are with us all day until mentoring," she says, smiling and putting her arm around my shoulder. "I'm sure you will be told where to go for mentoring, but now we go to lunch." Finally, something I know I can be hateful about. No school food is good.

"You are going to love the food here," Pres says, smiling. "It's amazing!" Well, so much for that. "Hope you like muffins." Valentine laughs as she and April make their way out. If I'm confused by that statement, it doesn't register because I hear a loud "CRUNCH," and I see Fall pulling a giant red apple out of his bag and taking a bite. He continues to eat it as we make our way down the hall. It doesn't seem feasible, but he has the apple finished by the time we get to the bottom of the stairs. Instead of turning right with the rest of us, he heads straight for a couch in the foyer.

"I told you," says Spring. "An extra hour of sleep." She again has looped her arm in mine, and we head toward the cafeteria. A line is forming. However, it moves quickly, and we soon enter. I'm angry because the smell is divine. How in the world are they able to get every great food smell into one great scent. Pres must have been reading my face.

"Smells great, doesn't it?" he says.

"Unreal," I reply.

We move forward, and I follow their lead and grab a tray. I look up to see a curly haired guy with chubby cheeks standing behind the food. He is decked out in a red chef's uniform.

"Hey, Muffin," Pres says. "How are you today?'

"Oh! Mister President! I'm overjoyed! We have the most magnificent food choices for you!" Muffin exclaims in a weird accent that isn't quite Russian, but also not French and with maybe even a bit of British in there, too. I have no clue. I look down in front of him, and all I see are muffin-shaped offerings.

"Don't be afraid," Spring says. "The Muffin Man only knows how to make food in muffin shapes, but trust me, they are all good." Looking up at Muffin, she explains, "Muffin, this is Arbor Day. She's new, and this is her first time dining with you." You would have thought Muffin had just won the lottery.

"OH BOY-O!" He shouts, hands raised over his head. "Your first time! Welcome, welcome, welcome, welcome, Arbor Day. Today is such a great day. We have garlic chicken muffins, potato muffins, and my famous vegetable medley muffin. Please, please do enjoy this meal." With that he places three muffins on a plate and practically tosses it to me. I take it and follow along after Pres and Spring.

I'm led to the side, where I pick up my drink. I'm happy to see that no matter what school you go to, the chocolate milk is always in the same carton. I take two and am led to a table off to the side where three other students are already seated. I smile as one of them is Columbus.

"Yes! I get to sit with the new holiday," says a young, dark-skinned boy with curly black hair. He seems super excited. He must love the school because he's decked out in HH gear from head to toe. HH hat. HH shirt. HH shorts. He is smaller and younger than the rest of us.

"Arbor, this is Flag," Pres tells me. "Also, with the last name Day. He is only 11, but he's a certified genius. Also, he really, really likes Holiday High."

"Are you kidding?" Flag pipes up. "I LOVE it here! Isn't it just the best school you have ever been to, Arbor?"

I look at that cute little face, and I don't have the heart to say otherwise. Luckily, I don't have to.

"You already know Columbus, and this here is Shadow," Spring says as I check out another girl sitting at the end. She has long dark hair and is writing in a dark red notebook. She's wearing a long, dark green slim dress that goes all the way from her neck down to her feet. She doesn't register that I'm there. "Shadow?" I ask.

"Well, technically, her name is Groundhog," offers up Columbus. "But she's a Major, so she can go by anything she wants, so she chose Shadow since she likes winter." Calmly, Shadow looks up at me.

"Are you kidding?" Shadow says. "I LOVE it. Isn't winter just the best thing ever?"

We all laugh, even Flag. I'm going to really like this girl. So glad she's living next to me.

I bring my attention back to my plate. Three muffins are staring back at me, and I can't wrap my head around the fact that this is my food. No one else is even hesitating. They all dig in. Spring finally notices and cracks a smile.

"Just take one bite," she says. I wish she hadn't because now the whole table pauses and looks at me. I never thought I would say this, but I pick up my fork and take a bite of chicken muffin.

"Oh my goodness," I say, eyes bulging out. I swallow and proclaim, "That's the best thing I've ever tasted!"

I wish I was lying. But wow. The chicken is so moist and juicy. Next, I dig into the potatoes and veggies. This is fabulous. Again, I find myself torn because I'm not supposed to like anything here. It's supposed to be awful—stupid Holiday High and their awesome food.

The rest of lunch is fun. I listen to Flag and Pres discuss changes the school has made. Apparently everyone got new mattresses and they are "The best beds ever," according to Flag.

Columbus, Shadow, and Spring fill me in on some of the other groups in the school. The main table they focus on is what they call "The Big Four." Even though there are really five of them. "The Big Four are Christmas, Easter, Halloween, and Thanksgiving. They always sit together. Fourth is part of The Big Four, but they kept the same name like college football conferences do. Only Valentine and April are allowed to be with them," explains Columbus.

I glance up and see Valentine feeding Santa grapes while April looks bored. With them is a big guy wearing a red shirt and green shorts with red sandals. No socks. He seems to be just focused on his food and not really into the conversation. There are three other students there, too. One is a girl dressed in what seems like a green angel costume, and the other guy's uniform is a mess. His sweater is on backward, and he has one sock pulled up and one pulled down with two different shoes on. That's an odd bunch. Last, there is a red-headed boy with a dog, but I never quite get the story on him.

"Now, who do we have here?" Comes a booming voice behind me. I jolt so much that I spit out a piece of my veggie muffin. I turn, and standing there is a seven-foot-tall giant with jet-black hair and beard. He is wearing a tight green shirt that reads "COACH" on it in white. Super tight sweatpants enclose his massive tree trunk legs and he has a red whistle hanging around his neck.

"Um," I stutter. "I'm Arbor Day."

"Well, I'll be!" exclaims the Coach as he slaps me on the back, almost knocking me off my chair. "I'm Coach Bunyan! Glad you're here!" My eyes feel like they are dilating from his booming voice. I'm just catching my breath when Bunyan announces, "Lunch is over, folks! Move it along."

I follow everyone's lead. We drop off our trays and head out. I'm relieved that Spring doesn't loop our arms together this time. The rest of the afternoon moves by fairly quickly. I thankfully avoid any more tense interactions with Valentine and April. Science seems like it will be fine. Mother Nature, or Mother, is quite eccentric with her long gray hair and green flowery dress, and she announces the science fair coming up soon, and against my better judgment, I get excited.

Calm but awkward is how I would describe P.E. Today, all Coach Bunyan talked about was the different ways we're going to improve our bodies this year. I can honestly say I never knew there were so many ways that one could strengthen their calf muscles. We have P.E. and Art with Track 1. Columbus, Shadow, Flag, and Santa are all part of Track 1, along with the red-headed kid and his dog.

I finally found out his name is Fourth, and his dog is his emotional assistance animal/therapy pet. Apparently, Fourth has a temper problem. The little white dog is named Pop. Anytime Fourth starts to pop, Pop will yip at him, and it's supposed to warn him to calm down. The last person in Track 1 is a slim Asian girl named J.J., and J.J. loves America. She's the school's only foreign exchange student, and her holiday is Chinese New Year. But she's from Taiwan—not China—there is a difference, and she will be sure to tell you all about it if you make the mistake of thinking she's Chinese. We head out of P.E., and I find Frost standing outside the door.

"You will come with me right now for your mentoring period," he says, greeting us all with a cold blast. My stomach drops, and I feel my face get red. You have got to be kidding me. I'm going to be mentored by Frost? He takes off without another word, and I have no choice but to follow. Spring and Pres give me a pained look as I depart.

We trek across the foyer and over to the other side, where the faculty offices are. I can't even imagine what Frost's office is going to be like. An igloo, maybe? Perhaps he will have a hole cut in the floor where we can ice fish. Just when I'm thinking about how to properly bait a hook with freezing hands, Frost stops. We are here, again, in front of Fairy's office.

"For some reason, Principal Fairy has chosen you for mentoring this year," he turns with a sniff and speaks softly. "If it was up to me, you would spend the year being mentored by Muffin. You look like you're well suited for scrubbing pots and pans." With that he takes off back down the hall, thankfully, giving me time to warm up. I knock on the door.

"Come in," sings a high voice. I go in and see that Fairy is already standing to the side of her desk with a whiteboard standing on an easel. It sure looks like she's ready to teach me something. I'm fine with that. I will learn anything from her, which sounds great after the fear of sitting under the tutelage of Frost. I sit down relieved. "So, like, what do we do now?" I ask.

"Well, first, Arbor, we wait for the other student to arrive," she says. I didn't know what mentoring was, but I guess I assumed it would be just me. I start going through the list of students I've met today, hoping beyond hope that neither Valentine nor April is the other mentee, when a knock at the door snaps me back to the present.

"Oh! There he is right now," Fairy joyfully announces. He? I turn around and coming into her office is Santa.

Chapter Six

My defenses are instantly up. Not only am I not used to being in a close setting with a guy my age, but I really don't want any more problems with Valentine. Santa is part of The Big Four. I want nothing to do with them. Now, I'm going to be stuck here every day for an hour and a half with one of them? I have nothing against Christmas except for the fact that it's over-commercialized, overshadows three months of the year, takes itself way too seriously, and, oh yeah, the whole, "We are about presents and not Jesus" thing.

"Am I late, Fairy?" Santa asks, coming in and grabbing the seat next to me. I don't think he notices, but he's totally sitting way too close to me. "I was talking to Coach about how to improve my calf muscles and lost track of time."

"Santa, you're right on time," Fairy says. "This is Arbor. She will be joining us this year in mentoring." Santa is already sitting too close, so I really hope he isn't a hugger like everyone else in this school seems to be. Well, except Frost, thank goodness. But luckily, Santa had no such plans.

"We haven't met yet," Santa says, reaching for my hand. I shake it only because it would be really awkward if I didn't. I try to give a firm shake, but I'm clearly no match for his grip. Maybe Coach Bunyan has some exercises for my hands.

"Hello, I'm Arbor," I reply.

"I'm Santa. Ho! Ho! Ho!" he replies back to me. It takes a second before I realize that he's joking. It tickles me, and I let out a laugh before I can catch it.

"Glad you got that," Santa smiles at me. He really needs to stop being nice. It's going to be hard to hate him if he's charming. I'm already intrigued to find out why he's dating someone like Valentine.

"Ok. Arbor and Santa, let's get started," says Fairy, moving to the front of the desk where she plants herself. "I first want to talk about why I have chosen you. As you know, each faculty member chooses two to three students to mentor each year. Sometimes, it can be a bit of a fight over who gets whom, but I want you to know that I get first choice on which students I mentor since I'm the head of the Holiday Council. I chose the both of you for very good reasons."

The familiar frustration boils up in me again. I remind myself again that Holiday High isn't important to me. I don't want to be here, and I will not give in to the pressure of changing what I believe my holiday should be. Even though I'm the first pick of the head of the Holiday Council, I won't be honored by this. Okay, I will be honored a little bit, but that's all.

"I have to admit," starts Santa. "I thought I would be with Coach again this year. Fall, Columbus, and I were hoping to get extra work in for baseball season in the spring."

"You have spent enough time with Coach Bunyan," Fairy explains. "This year, it's going to be very beneficial to you and our school that you spend time with me."

"Why is that?" Santa says, confused. I, too, am interested in finding out why and how I relate to this.

"Santa, I want you to listen to me closely," Fairy says, looking very serious. "Your holiday is the top holiday in our country. Everything begins with the success of Christmas. I've met with your parents, and they are concerned that you're focusing more on sports than the future of the holiday." I notice right away that Santa starts to shift in his seat and wring his hands together. The relaxed nature in which he was sitting earlier is now replaced with stiffness and anxiety.

"In fact, we had a rather serious meeting over the summer," Fairy continues. "Your father has decided you're no longer to play baseball this year." With that statement, I look into Santa's eyes. No longer is he the playful "Ho! Ho! Ho!" guy. All I see is a distant look of pain. I continue to sit there feeling uncomfortable about being part of what is obviously a serious family issue.

"Santa," Fairy says gently. "There is no reason to worry. I agreed to take you on in my mentoring class, and they agreed that if that were to happen, then you would be able to still be part of the team in the spring. That's why you're here with us right now."

"I don't understand," Santa whispered softly. "How is my playing ball going to affect the future of the holiday?"

"Your father's concern is that you pour so much energy and effort onto the baseball field that you neglect to give some of that to your studies. Remember this, Santa, you're the future of the holiday. Your future does not lie on the diamond but back home at Pole."

Santa looks like a withered leaf. I've seen many times that when a leaf reaches the end of the autumn cycle, it finally loses its strength and lets go. It will fall to the ground, thus completing its life, and goes back to the earth. It's hard to see someone born in the mold of Viking greatness look so broken.

"This is a good thing, Santa," Fairy says, gently putting her hand on his shoulder. "We are going to take this year, and you're going to be the best thing that could have ever happened to Christmas. Look into my eyes." Santa looks up, and I notice the warmth and glow growing around our Principal. "I believe in you. You are a gifted and talented young man. When we're done, your father will never doubt your ability to lead this holiday again."

Santa starts to sit up straighter, and even I feel more belief in him. Not knowing what to do in this intimate moment, I use the only tool I know to use. I make a joke.

"You will do great," I say. "Even I will want to sit on your lap and ask for presents." Both Fairy and Santa look at me. For a moment, I think I said the worst thing that could have been said, but both Fairy and Santa start to laugh, and I feel the tension ease.

"You promise?" Santa says, and I see that his face has started to shift back to its happy position. I start to blush instantly.

"Now, Arbor," starts Fairy addressing me. "Why are you here with us?"

"I'm wondering the same thing," I answer. "If Christmas is the top holiday, then why am I here? Arbor Day was just deemed worthy. Shouldn't another one of the Big Four be in here with you?"

With that being said, I see Fairy's eyes intensify. Uh oh. I'm for sure out of this school now. But isn't that what I want? Why am I feeling dread right now? Is this what getting hugs does? Make you start to care about things you aren't supposed to care about.

"Arbor, the fact that you're not a Big Four is the exact reason you're in here," Fairy explains. "The gap between the Minors and Majors grows wider with each and every year." She pauses. "There are some on the Holiday Council who would like to see the Majors be the only ones that benefit from this magical place we call Holiday High. We are going to take this year and show them that the Minor and Major holidays have more in common than they think. We are going to shrink that gap."

I sit in stunned silence. Why is she doing this with me? I don't even want to be here. I'm trying to find every reason I can to hate this place, and now, I'm going to have this pressure to bring the holidays together. No, thank you! I didn't ask for this. Any of it.

"Now, you look at me, Arbor," Fairy says, obviously reading

my face. I look up. Despite the anger inside, I do feel the warmth covering me.

"I've thought long and hard about this. Your holiday was chosen for a reason. When I met with your parents, I was told about a girl who is wise beyond her years, but also a girl who has no belief in that wisdom and would rather live behind a wall of sarcasm than to embrace the talent with which she has been blessed. I'm going to help you embrace that talent this year."

Turning back to Santa, she continued, "All three of us here are going to put Holiday High and the council on notice." Inspiration hits me, and I know she's close to selling me on this. "Santa, you're going to show everyone how capable you are of continuing the legacy of Christmas. Arbor, you're going to show everyone at the Confirmation that the Minor holidays are the foundation of celebration. Arbor Day is going to be taken to new heights. I believe when they see that you two are working together...." She pauses.

"No, not just working together. When they see you supporting each other and treating each other as equals, anyone who thinks the separation of Majors and Minors needs to continue will face so much opposition that they will let go of any old-fashioned superiority they feel is right."

"I promised my parents that I would try hard," I say. I take time to think about what to say next. I did come here to change the system and to make Holiday High different than it has ever been. Here is the top person offering me that very chance. I wouldn't even have to do it on my own. So here we go. Things are going to be different from this point on.

"I promise you that I will try hard," I finally say. A big smile comes across Fairy's face and the glow behind her intensifies. She pats me on the leg and speaks.

"And I promise you, Arbor, I will work hard for you--both of you." She says, looking at Santa. "But it's very important that both of you know that you can't speak of this or what you learn in here to anyone. Not to your parents, your friends, or the other faculty here. It's imperative that you understand that."

"I do," I say nodding. We both look at Santa. "I do, too," he offers.

But looking at me, "Are you really down to do this Arbor?." I feel a swell in my chest as his blue eyes look into mine. For a moment, I don't mind that he's sitting so close.

"I also promise you that I will try hard," I say, hoping he believes me. "Good."

He smiles. "Then, when this is done, I may just sit on your lap, too."

CHAPTER SEVEN

I can't sleep. After the mentoring time, all I can think is: How can I help Fairy make the Minor holidays more important? I left her office in a daze. My head was full of all she had shared and the fact that Santa is nothing like I would have guessed. I can't believe the pressure that his father is putting on him. Sure, my parents pressured me to come here, but they would never stop me from participating in something that I love in order to better suit the holiday. I also marvel at how twenty-four hours can change one's outlook on things. I silently curse myself for giving in to the school's charm.

Dinner was another great experience. Not only did I find out spaghetti can be made in muffin form, but I spent the whole meal listening to stories about Holiday High. I'm especially tickled when I hear about Pres' fumbling attempt at courtship last year. He seemed intent on asking out New Year's last year. Not only did he trip and fall all over the place, but she didn't even understand what he was trying to ask.

"I can speak formally all day long to my friends, but the moment I try to be smooth, it's like my tongue swells, and I can't speak," He explains, turning a bright shade of red. I look around trying to locate this love of his, but then they explain to me that she's in Taiwan this year while J.J. is here.

"Maybe you can better tell her how you feel through a letter," I offer. "That way, you can take your time and say it perfectly."

"That's an excellent idea, Arbor," Spring chimes in. "Plus, a lady always loves a heartfelt letter."

"Yeah. You can get some nicely scented pink paper and write a LOVE poem," Shadow adds.

We all laugh, but I see something click in Pres' eyes. Perhaps he will actually write her a letter. It felt nice to have your peers listen to you. I didn't have much of that in my old school.

That night, Spring took it upon herself to gather the ladies of our table in my room. So Spring, Columbus, Shadow, and I spent the night talking about the essay due on Friday, how to keep Fall awake more, and the back-to-school bonfire scheduled for Saturday.

"The bonfire is so much fun," Spring says.

"Sure, if you like the outdoors, being hot, and smelling like smoke for the rest of the week—not to mention the bugs!" Shadow adds, falling over in despair.

"I've never been to one," I say. The looks of the three girls are of disbelief. I go on to explain to them that I wasn't much of a social butterfly at my previous school. I always was content to go home after school and just stay in my own world.

"Well, not anymore," Spring says, hopping on the bed with me. "You are my sister now." Columbus hops up and gives Shadow a look. Shadow sighs and climbs on, too.

"I've always wanted a sister," Spring continues. "Fall is great, but all he cares about are sports and sleep." We all chuckle. She takes my hand in hers, and Columbus grabs my other. With another look and sigh, Shadow grabs Columbus' other hand. "I'm so glad you're here, Arbor. Not only was I sick of being the only Minor girl in our Track, but you're simply divine."

They finally leave, and I get ready for bed. I'm not surprised to find that Holiday High has provided me with red and green sleep-wear. The HH logo is going to haunt my dreams. I just know it!

Thus, here I am. Lying in the most comfortable bed that I've ever been in and I can't sleep. My thoughts won't shut down, and I don't want to dig my headphones out of my trunk. I finally give up and decide to use this time for good. I pull on some sweats and head down to the study lounge. Checking the clock, I notice it's half past eleven. I turn out of the hallway to go downstairs when I'm stopped right in my tracks. Standing before me is a short figure in red pajamas.

"Who are you? Where are you going? Why are you out of bed?" This figure questions me. He speaks so fast I can barely understand him. I look closely and see he has light golden skin with dizzyingly blue eyes. He is carrying a lantern that also seems to be an hourglass.

"I'm Arbor. I'm going to the study lounge. I couldn't sleep," I answer him back.

"Arbor, you say? New Student? New Holiday? Here at my school?" Pajama man says, getting more excited.

"Yes, I said Arbor. I'm a new student. I'm an old holiday but new to your new school." I say, giving him the information he was seeking. I wonder if this is some kind of night ninja I'm going to have to fight to get downstairs.

"Good, good, good," the Pajama Man says, clapping. "I'm Sandman. I keep eyes on the school at night. Study Lounge go. Boys side, no." Sandman moves out of the way and lets me pass down the stairs. I hurriedly move down to the first floor and head to the lounge. Sandman seems more like a hyperactive child than a scary night watchman, but I don't want to run the risk of getting in trouble my first night here.

I feel relieved when I make it into the lounge. That's before I notice I'm not alone. I can't even believe someone else is in here. The lounge is equipped with six tables and chairs in the middle. The room is ringed by couches and giant oversized recliners arranged on every wall. Sitting at one of the tables is a boy with red hair. He is wearing all green and glasses. He has headphones on, so I approach slowly. He still doesn't seem to notice I'm coming. I gently knock on the table. Still, he doesn't look up. I start waving my hand, hoping he will eventually notice there is someone else in the room, but he's so into his work he still doesn't look up. So I walked around the table and tapped him on the shoulder.

"AYE!!!!!!!!!!" The red-headed boy screams. I jump back, shocked at his reaction. He starts to breathe fast and holds his hands to his chest. Shaking his head, he looks down at the table. "I'm so sorry," I say, moving away and over to another table.

"No, no. It's okay," he says, starting to calm down. "I get so lost in my own mind. I had no idea you came in." He takes his headphones out and stops his music. I see he's working on the math assignment Old Man had given us earlier. "How about I don't scream this time and just say, 'Hello, I'm Patrick.'" "Well, then, I won't scream, either. I'm Arbor, and again, I'm so sorry. I generally don't make a habit of scaring people." I connect the dots and realize that he's a Major—St. Patrick's Day. I can't remember seeing him at all today.

"Ah, Arbor Day," he says, smiling. "I heard we had a new holiday. I was late for school today. My family spent the summer overseas, and we just returned. We went to visit family and to do some research."

"Wow, I bet that was fascinating," I say, revealing too much jealousy. "I always wanted to go overseas." I feel a twinge of anger. Major holidays have way more resources at their disposal than Minor holidays do.

"It was...." he pauses, "... eye-opening in many ways." He goes silent. I start to see a deep thought form behind his eyes. I sit there quietly for a bit before I pull up my bag and start to unload my notebooks. That seems to snap him out of it. "You are more than welcome to join me here at the table," he says, motioning to the chair across from me. "I don't usually have company this late in the lounge." I get up and move to the table across from him.

"I couldn't sleep," I explain. "Today has been overwhelming. Also, I have no idea what I'm going to write for this essay in Grimm's class." He starts to laugh.

"Well," he says, pointing at me. "You have come to the right person. You see, Grimm loves a happy ending. No matter what you put down, as long as your holiday comes out on the top and you're thrilled, you're golden."

"Good to hear," I say. That's when I notice he's wearing a necklace with a shamrock on it. "That's odd," I say. "Why are you wearing a shamrock necklace? Isn't your family against it?" He glances up from his work with a strange look on his face. "I'm sorry. I didn't mean to offend you. I had just read your father didn't like the shamrock as a symbol for your holiday."

"Oh, I would say he still doesn't like it," Patrick says, smiling at me. "Much to his anguish, I acquired this over the summer. I actually thought he might get customs to prevent me from re-entering the country."

"Why?" I ask. He looks at me quizzically, and I explain more. "I mean, why doesn't he like the symbol, and why are you wearing it now?"

"That, Arbor Day, is too long of a story for tonight." I don't know if it's my imagination, but I think I see a flicker of pain flit across his face. I wonder, again, if I'm getting a glimpse into the world of a Major Holiday not many people get to see or would want people to see. From the outside, it looks like the Majors have all the advantages in our world. For one, their children don't have to face the Confirmation each year. That alone would be less stressful for any Minor. Majors always seem so sure of themselves, so confident in their decisions, but after seeing Santa this afternoon and Patrick here, I wonder how much of it's a façade.

"So..." I say, changing the subject, "Grimm likes happy?" He refocuses and smiles. "Seems kind of ironic, doesn't it?" We both laugh as we get to work. I start a basic outline of the happiest scenario I can think of for my holiday. My parents get more funding. They get to travel to all the major forests in the country. We travel overseas to see how they celebrate the holiday in other countries and school programs all over, dedicating weeks to the study and planting of trees. Songs written, shows produced, shirts printed. I giggle at the thought of green shirts everywhere. The more I work on this outline, the more it switches from something happy to please Grimm into something that I really would like to happen. Maybe that's the point.

Before I know it, the clock strikes one A.M. "You hungry?" Patrick asks. He is rubbing the palms of his hands on his cheeks. "I'm starving." "Me, too," I sigh. "But where are we going to get food at this time of night?" He starts to chuckle at me. I don't know if I like him laughing at a perfectly reasonable question.

"We just go next door to the cafeteria," He says with a smirk. "But we aren't allowed in there except for mealtimes," I counter back, starting to get a little suspicious. "Let me guess," he says, starting to laugh, "Frost gave you his tour?"

"He sure did. It was chilling. I'm not about to start my tenure here on the bad side of that man." "Frost is harmless—well, mostly," Patrick says back at me. "Well, you happen to be looking at Muffin's right-hand man." Now, it's my turn to smirk at him. Really? This red-headed bookworm is being mentored by Muffin? Wouldn't he be a better fit learning more about Science or Math?

"I see you're skeptical. Come on." Patrick stands up and starts towards the door. "I'm serious. Come on." He holds out his hand for me to take. I pause. Many thoughts run through my head, none of which are scarier than taking a guy's hand. A guy I just met. A stranger, really. All of a sudden, I'm aware of everything wrong with my hands. They are huge. My fingers are freakishly long. I didn't wash them before I came down. They feel clammy and wet.

"I'm perfectly fine to follow you," I say, getting up from my chair, shyly trying to wipe my hands on my sweats. "So, if you're Muffin's sous chef, how do you suppose we get in?"

Again, Patrick looks at me, laughing. This time, though, it's not a mean laugh—more of disbelief. "You really aren't trusting, are you, Arbor Day?" He opens the door, and I follow him into the hallway. "Wait," I whisper. "What about the Sandman?"

"Sandman?" He says, looking at me weirdly. "Who is that?" Now, it's my turn to look at him in disbelief. "You know the little guy who watches over the school at night. He makes sure we aren't up to no good." I continue to look at him. He gets those deep thoughts in his eyes again. "Arbor," he says, looking serious. "There is no night watchman." Suddenly, panic grips me. Who did I talk to? I start to look back down the hall, suddenly aware of how many dark shadows there are here. I turn back to Patrick for help and see him standing there with the cheesiest grin on his face.

"You JERK!" I holler a little too loud. I start slapping him on the arm. He puts his hands up in defense, laughing like crazy. UGH! The nerve of him. "Oh man, that was awesome!" He puts down his guard, but I'm still fuming. "Sandy is only concerned about us going to the third floor. If he comes by here, he will want some of the food. Not to get us in trouble." I stand there with my arms crossed. I don't like being fooled.

"But to answer your question," he says, crossing over to the door. "This is how we get it in." He stops in front of the door and reaches for the handle. He slowly opens it and looks back at me. "Magic," he whispers. This time, it's my turn to have a cheesy smile. "Whatever." I roll my eyes and follow him in.

The cafeteria is lit by the same small chandeliers that hang in the bedrooms upstairs and give off a nice glow. The room smells like the rest of the school. Tonight, I'm sensing a mix of vanilla and blueberries. I'm starting to understand the school knows what you like or need at that moment. It's almost like Holiday High is just as much alive and active as the people that inhabit it. That may explain why my fight to dislike it was futile. If it senses what you

47

like, then you will always be encountering pleasantness everywhere you go. Maybe it can change Frost? Valentine could use some work, too.

True to his word, Patrick makes his way back to the kitchen and emerges again with two giant muffins. He has also grabbed a couple of milk cartons. He makes his way to the center table and hops up. "On the table?" I ask. "Sure," he says.

He starts laying out the snack, and I move onto the table with all the grace I can manage. We are sitting cross-legged, facing each other. I admire the way he's taking care of the placement.

"Okay, Arbor," Patrick finally says after everything is set up between us. "This is going to be the best thing you have ever eaten. These are peanut butter, white chocolate, and banana muffins. The goal is that with every bite, you get a taste of everything." He slowly pushes my plate towards me. He is looking at me with eager eyes, so I break off a big piece and pop it into my mouth.

"Oh my word," I exclaim. I'm sure my eyes are popping out of my skull since my taste buds feel like they are popping off my tongue. Being the skeptic that I am, I can't believe what I tasted. Patrick wasn't lying. I taste the peanut butter instantly, but as I chew, the white chocolate and banana appear to make a perfect symphony in my mouth. "Wow," I mutter, mouth full of muffin. "This is amazing."

"Glad you like it," he says with the biggest smile. "It's my recipe." I swallow the last bite. "Really?" I say. "That's amazing, Patrick." He finally breaks a piece off and eats it. His eyes close, and a smile comes across his face. "Man, I missed that." We sit there, eating in silence a bit. With every bite, I'm amazed how good this muffin tastes.

"I made these last year during Mentoring," Patrick says, breaking the silence. "Muffin liked them so much he started making them regularly. Take a drink of milk with your next bite." I do what he says and marvel at how the white milk adds the final touch to the experience. He smiles at me again, obviously loving that I'm loving this. I wipe my mouth and take a break for a bit. "You said you missed it. What does that mean?" I ask. He starts to wipe the crumbs off his hands and takes a swig of his milk.

"My father thinks the culinary world is a waste of time," He says back to me. "We were together all summer and, well, there is no reason to really try to do anything else with Father but what he wants to do." He looks down and I see this saddens him. The intimacy of the moment hits me. Low lights, the food, the exposure of one's secrets. Something stirs in me, and I find myself wanting to be closer to him.

"I didn't want to come to Holiday High," I whisper to him. "My parents and I fought over it all summer." I go on to tell him all about my parents' wishes for me. How my father wanted to come so badly when he was my age but never had the chance. The promise I made to them. I feel more exposed now than if I was sitting here naked. "For what it's worth, I wish your father could taste this right here," I say. "Maybe then he can see how much this means to you." He lifts his head and closes his eyes. He smiles and lets out a big sigh.

"I don't think it would do any good. Father has his vision for our holiday, and I'm to follow that vision. He lets me assist Muffin when I'm here as long as I keep my grades perfect. Any slip up there and I'm not allowed within one hundred yards of the kitchen." I feel bad for him. I've never had any outside interests to pull me away from the holiday. Any and all attempts at dancing, sports, or musical instruments were all met with clumsiness and stage fright. But even if I did, I can't imagine my parents ever preventing me from participating in something I love. It doesn't seem fair that just because you were born into a rite of celebration it means you can have no other route but to focus your whole life on that.

"Thank you for sharing this with me, Patrick." I try to say this in the most sincere way I can without a trace of sarcasm or snarkiness. I plead with my eyes, hoping that he knows I truly mean what

I said. "Thank you, Arbor Day, for making my night most enjoyable and not at all what I expected." He smiles and starts to gather our stuff up from the table. We walk over, discard our wrappers and empty cartons in the garbage. Then walk back to the Study Lounge. Sleep suddenly starts to hit me hard, and I think I may just do my best impersonation of Fall and sleep on one of the couches. Instead, I slowly start packing my bag while Patrick does the same. "Every night," he says, throwing me off. "Huh?" I yawn. "I'm here every night," he says, taking my arm. "You are welcome to come keep me company."

The touch on my arm starts to tingle, and I wonder how long he's going to keep it there. "Fine," I reply. "Every night, I'm welcomed." He smiles and lets go of my arm, and we both head to our rooms.

Chapter Eight

I wake the next morning to loud pounding on my door. It takes me a while to register where I am and what the noise is. I didn't actually fall asleep until after two o'clock in the morning. It took me forever to calm down and process my time with Patrick. It's rare that I feel a strong connection with anyone, especially someone my age and a boy! Last night was like a dream. The closeness and openness shared was exhilarating and also scary. All these thoughts are swirling in my head as the pounding continues. I slowly sit up, rub my eyes and look at the clock: 7:00 A.M.

What in the world? Morning Assembly isn't until 9. I've mastered the art of getting up at the last minute and looking presentable. I could easily get it done in fifteen minutes. I groan and shuffle across the room. Someone is about to get the wrath of Arbor. I open the door and there are Columbus, Shadow, and Spring standing there in red robes, carrying their shower buckets.

"What the snot?" I ask them through tired eyes. They look at me like the problem is with me and not with the fact they are the crazy girls banging on my door. "Get your stuff, Arbor," Shadow says in a mix of command and question. I stand there dumbfounded. "Uh, guys, " I say. "Last night was great and all, but I don't really shower with others. It's more of a private thing?" I speak the last part as a question because I really have no clue what is going on at this point. Also, how does Spring look so good first thing in the morning? Did she even sleep?

"Trust us, " Spring says, coming into my room. "You will want to grab your things and come with us right now." She starts opening my wardrobe, looking through it until she pulls out a red robe, just like the others. When did I get that? Chalk one up for the magic school again. I cross the room and start gathering my supplies. "This is crazy. Why are we going to the showers so early?"

"We can talk about it on the way to the showers, " Spring says, pushing me out the door. The showers are located at the end of our hallway. "You'll see, if we don't get in there before Valentine, April, and the other girls, then there is going to be no more hot water, and the place will be a mess." Spring explains. I stop and all the girls turn and look at me. "So you're saying that I was woken up and dragged out here because all the other girls take too long?" Before I get an answer, Shadow grabs my arm and drags me the rest of the way. "This isn't a game." She stresses to me. "I don't know where you came from, but sharing four showers with this many girls is a combat sport." I continue to be dragged down the hall and through the bathroom doors. As it happens, we aren't even the first ones there.

"Good morning, fellow Holidays!" We are greeted by a chirpy and happy J.J. I step in and realize that I've entered the world of plush spas. Red velvet couches, four green porcelain sinks, and mirrors. J.J. seems to just be wrapping up as we're coming in. "Isn't this the most amazing bathroom you have ever seen?" she says. "In Taiwan, the bathroom is one big room. The shower and toilet are all together. But not here in America!" She's way too happy for this early in the morning. She finishes gathering her things, making sure to wipe every surface down clean. "You will have a great day!" She says and exits.

As soon as J.J. leaves, I make a beeline straight for one of the velvet couches. "Oh, no you don't," says Columbus, grabbing me. "We have a good solid thirty minutes in here before it becomes a war zone." I tug away. "Fine, wake me in twenty." But much to my chagrin, I'm foiled in my attempts for more rest. The girls lead me through the demonstration of how to operate the many bells and whistles of the showers. I'm not amazed when the water comes out at the perfect temperature since this school seems to be tuned into all my preferences. Once I'm done, I'm led through a whirlwind of more face washing, hair drying, and styling. "I usually just wear my hair down," I say to Spring. "Not today," she chimes as she pushes me in front of her. I don't know what those small magic hands do, but my hair ends up looking like something between a fairy and a tree. But I love it. Sure enough, we're just wrapping up and headed back down the hall as we pass Valentine and April making their way to the showers. We pass by and I feel their gazes land on me. I try to ignore their giggles as I'm returned to my room.

I gather my things and do a zombie walk down to join the others at breakfast. It's strange to see the cafeteria all lit up and busy this morning. The memories of last night flood into my mind. I find myself getting nervous at the thought of seeing Patrick this morning. I don't really know why this is bothering me. All we did was study and share a muffin and nothing more.

But my stomach still feels wobbly. With those thoughts swirling around, I get in line and find myself standing behind Fall. Muffin hands him his breakfast while we're still in line, and he starts to eat it right away. I'm handed a plate with my muffin and look up to see Patrick grinning. "Good Morning, Arbor," he says. "Hope you enjoy our bacon, egg, and cheese muffin." I stand there staring at him for what seems like an hour before I mumble something that resembles a thank you. I rush along, horrified. Why am I acting so weird?

I grab my milk and head to the table where everyone seems to be seated. Fall, it seems, has already finished his muffin and is napping. Shadow is writing in her notebook, nibbling on the muffin. Columbus and Spring are chatting about the bonfire while Flag and Pres are in a deep debate over the exact way Muffin gets the egg, cheese, and bacon ratio correct. All seem too deeply engrossed in what they are doing, which is why I think what happens next comes as such a shock.

"Mind if I sit here?" I look up to see Patrick setting his tray down and taking the seat next to me. The way everyone stops and looks, you would think Patrick has a third arm or four eyes. Spring is the one that recovers the quickest.

"Why, good morning, Patrick!" she says in a way too happy voice. The others seem still frozen. I'm not sure how to act. So in typical Arbor fashion, I say the first thing that comes to my mind.

"Why are you sitting here?" Oh boy. Really, Arbor? Patrick starts to laugh, and I'm instantly relieved. "I needed a break to eat and I figure this as good of a place as any, He says, smiling. He looks around at the rest of the table, still staring at him.

"You're St. Patrick's Day," Flag whispers. Patrick chuckles. "Yes, I am. And you're Flag." Flag's eyes start to widen and a grin breaks across his face. "I *am* Flag! Welcome to our table, St. Patrick's Day. This is Pres; that's Columbus and Shadow and Spring. That there is Fall. Fall is asleep, as you can see." I've never seen anyone so excited to have someone sit at a table before. Patrick handles the excitement in stride. "Thanks Flag! Now I know who everyone is."

"So, Arbor, did you sleep well after last night?" he says, turning back to me. Now, it's Spring's turn for her eyes to widen. I glance quickly around the table. Columbus looks confused, and Shadow wears a sly smile on her face. This is horrifying. I know that as soon as we get alone, I'm going to have some explaining to do with the girls. Patrick must have seen the looks because he continues on. "Arbor had trouble sleeping last night," he explains, taking a bite to eat. "She came down to the study lounge and distracted me from my work." I roll my eyes. Distracted isn't the word I would use.

Before I can explain more and wipe that grin off Shadow's face, the bell rings. I have literally been saved by the bell. We start to gather our things while Spring shakes Fall awake. He looks up and surveys where he is. His eyes stop on Patrick. "Okay," he says and gets up with the rest of us.

The rest of the day is calm. The morning assembly was a presentation on war and how it affects holidays. It was led by Frost. "He always has the most awful topics, " Spring whispers to me. Thankfully, Patrick sat with some of the other Majors and I was spared any more embarrassment. In fact, day two was crazy busy and there was no time to speak. Any time Spring got a chance to corner me about Patrick, I was able to weasel my way out of it. Before I knew it, I was on my way to Mentoring. When I arrived at Fairy's office, she and Santa were already inside.

"Hello, Arbor." Fairy greets me as I walk in. Santa looks way more relaxed than when we left yesterday. There is no marker board today. I wonder if there has been a change in plans and Santa is going back to Coach Bunyan. I don't want to go back to Bunyan. Today we had an hour of lifting a medicine ball and tossing it. Well, I actually had an hour of *trying* to lift a medicine ball. It finally turned into rolling the medicine ball. At least I wasn't alone. Flag barely moved it. But then again, Flag is eleven. Man, I'm weak. I settle in my seat and pull a notebook out.

"No need for a notebook today, Arbor," Fairy explains as she takes a seat behind her desk. "Today, I just want to talk. We can't work together if we don't understand and trust each other. The only way that can happen is if we open up in here. Can you two do that for me? Open up and try to understand each other?" I take a deep breath. Fairy might as well have asked me to perform open heart surgery. Last night, notwithstanding, I don't generally enjoy being open and honest about my feelings. Fairy may be sitting there looking at the both of us with the most earnest of faces, but all I feel is tired. I risk a look at Santa. He seems to be taking this in stride. Maybe he's used to baring his soul to people. His whole game is knowing if I'm naughty or nice, anyway. Perhaps I can't hide anything from him to begin with. But if honesty is what Fairy wants, I might as well start with the most honest thing I can think of.

"I don't like being open and honest," I say. With that comment, Santa starts to laugh. I shoot him a look. Really? That's the reaction that I'm going to get for being honest?

"No, no, no," Santa says. "I'm only laughing because I was thinking the exact same thing." I continue to look at him, not really knowing how to respond. "Honest." He adds. "Arbor," Fairy addresses me. "The fact that you know that about yourself is a good thing."

"It means, for both of you, that when you get to the point when you truly open up and trust each other, then it's going to be real and genuine. I cannot stress to you two enough that we will not be successful this year if we're not genuine." With that, she pauses. For the first time since I've met Fairy, a smile isn't on her face. The look now is one of tiredness. I start to ponder what it's like to be her. Not only is she taxed with overseeing the school and the safety of the students. But she's the head of the Holiday Council, a job that I'm starting to sense is more complicated than I could ever dream.

"Will you do the same for us, Fairy?" I snap out of it at the sound of Santa's voice. "Will you be open and honest with us, too?" I'm intrigued by his question. This is a good point. Santa has secretly scored a point with me. Fairy takes a moment to consider, and slowly, the smile returns to her face.

"Santa, I believe that in order for you two to open up to me, I also need to open up to you," Fairy explains. "This is a team. Remember this and don't forget it. I chose you two for a reason. Please choose me, too. Choose me as someone that you can trust." We all sit in silence for a bit. I feel a heaviness in the room. My shoulders are stiff, and I sort of feel like I'm swimming through something thick. My emotions have been stretched to the limit over the past 48 hours. I start to run a checklist in my head.

Fear, Anger, Love, Excitement, Doubt, Worry, Joy. Something clicks, and I think this is something that Fairy would like shared. "If I'm being honest." I start. "I'm overwhelmed. The whole journey here has been a struggle. I barely walked through the doors yesterday morning. Then the school smelled nice, my room was great, I met Spring, I ate great muffins, I missed my parents, I couldn't sleep last night, and I had to shower with four other girls." I stop so I can catch my breath. I look up and Fairy is laughing.

"Oh, Arbor, I can't imagine what you're going through. Perhaps I've come on too strong for the second day," Fairy offers. "I forget that you're new here and are still trying to assimilate into this new stage of life. Please forgive that." I appreciate Fairy's words, but at the same time, I'm frustrated by them. I want to help her. "If it helps at all," Santa states. "I'm here to help." I look at him. The blue eyes, the long white hair. Could this really be an ally for me?

"I want to talk about the Rite of Celebration," Fairy says, addressing the both of us. "What does the Rite of Celebration mean to you?" The Rite of Celebration has been something I'm sure we have both learned about since an early age. I feel confident that this is something I can answer.

"The Rite of Celebration is the responsibility that we have to continue the legacy of our holiday. It means that we're the future. Our holiday rests with us," I explain. Fairy turns and looks at Santa. "It means that it's all up to us. We learn, we grow, and we take the holiday's responsibility when our parents deem it time. It's our Rite of Celebration. We were born into this." We both pause and look at Fairy. She smiles. "Let's get to work."

CHAPTER NINE

The rest of the week sets into a routine. Classes start to feel more familiar, and I get accustomed to my surroundings. All is better than I could have ever expected, minus the fact that each morning starts with banging on my door. I have tried to avoid Patrick as much as I can. The girls have finally stopped pestering me, and he seems to have gone back to sitting with the other Majors. He was not there on the first day, but apparently, he usually eats at the Big Four table with Santa, Valentine, and the others. Despite being up each night, I have not ventured back to the study lounge.

Mentoring continues to be an anomaly to me. I often leave more discouraged than anything. We learn that there are many leaders amongst the Major holidays that want the Minors to take even more of a backseat. I'm floored to learn that I was barely admitted to attend this year. It seems that a vote of 4-3 is what gave me this chance. Fairy tells me time and time again not to worry about what has been done in the past. Focus on proving them wrong and making it better for any other Minor holidays to get deemed worthy. Santa even seems dumbfounded at times.

He knows where his father stands on the issue and it seems to me that he's embarrassed by the whole situation. I try my hardest to be open and honest, but I'm too angry to really get a good grasp on the words I want to say.

I'm thankful when Saturday arrives. I make it very clear to Spring that I DO NOT wish to be woken up at 7 a.m. and that I look forward to getting some alone time. The problem with going from my life into the close surroundings of Holiday High is that my introverted tree needs to be watered. If I don't get time to myself, I tend to become even more withdrawn. After much discussion, I was promised that I would be excused from any plans until we had lunch. The girls gave me a goofy guilt trip that I would be missing a wonderful morning of streaming movies. But alone time is what I needed. So when I heard a knock at my door at 9 A.M. I was beyond annoyed.

I remove myself from the comfy chair and my warm blanket. Grumbling across the room I can't help but think about how much I love Spring, but this is getting crazy. I throw open the door and standing there is Valentine. Well, that was not who I was expecting. I just stand there, not really knowing how to handle this. What is she doing here?

"Are you going to invite me in?" she asks. I peek outside, expecting to see her little sidekick, but she's alone. Valentine continues to stand there. In my mind, I'm trying to figure out how to handle this situation, but honestly, I never thought I would have a time when Valentine would be gracing me with her presence. "My goodness, Arbor, you're hopeless," Valentine says, pushing past me and into my room. So yeah, Valentine is now in my room. Not exactly how I saw this morning going. She takes in her surroundings. "This isn't bad," she offers. "Not exactly what I would go for. Too ... earthy." I've only caught glimpses of Valentine's room as I passed by. Her room can be summed up in one word: hearts. They were everywhere. So, her calling my room earthy is a compliment and I will take it.

"Ok," she says, turning around. "We need to talk." She looks at me like I'm the one that needs to start the conversation. But she's the one that knocked on my door. I'm racking my brain trying to figure out what in the world Valentine would need to talk to me about. Suddenly, I find myself wishing I was streaming movies with the others. Or at least that Columbus was here. I think Valentine finally realizes that I'm not going to be electing to speak anytime soon.

"Santa is my boyfriend," she starts by saying. Well, this isn't a shocker to me. It's pretty common knowledge. "I know him better than anyone in this school and this past week, he has been acting strange." I process this information through the filter of Fairy's guidance. Santa and I have been dealing with some real issues in mentoring, and it's not surprising that Valentine has picked up on that.

"I need to know what is going on in mentoring," she continues. "Every day, when he comes out of there, he's silent and distant. I ask him what is going on and he draws even further away." She steps closer to me. Her dark eyes seem to focus clearly on my face. "What is going on in there?" Besides what Valentine may think at this moment I'm not intimidated by her. The fact that she's in here shows that she's worried about something, and, therefore, she needs me to get the answers. She can't just waltz in here and be demanding. Not in my own room.

"Valentine," I say, incredibly impressing myself with how calm I'm being. "I cannot and will not tell you what goes on in mentoring. If Santa has chosen not to tell what is happening when we meet with Fairy, then there is no way I'm going to tell you." She does not like this answer. I can see the wheels turning as she's processing what to say.

"You are new here, Arbor," she replies back. "So I'm going to clue you in on some things." I wish she would back away some because when someone is this close to me for this long of a time, I tend to start getting angry. Especially if they are speaking to me in a way that I don't like. Valentine is pushing me and I sure hope I don't start pushing back.

"Something you need to know is that Minors need to be respectful of us Majors. You are here as our guests. Minors, at the very best, are just an accessory to us." She pauses to let her words sink in. I'm instantly grateful to Fairy and her mentoring time. For the past week, she has given me insight into this theory that the Majors have. Now I know exactly what it looks like.

"So when I come to you or any other Major comes to you, make sure you're giving us the respect due." Valentine backs up a little. She takes a long look at me. "So," she says, twisting some of my hair in her hand. "I'm going to ask you this one more time." I jerk away from her. This makes her smile. "What happens in mentoring with you and Santa?" Now, it's my time to take a long look at her. Standing before me is someone trying hard to look and be tough.

"Valentine," I start to say when something clicks and I smile. I know who Valentine's mentor is, and this is the perfect opportunity for such action. She's a disciple of Frost. I'm repulsed. I straighten my shoulders and peer down. "You will leave my room right now. You will not ask me any more questions. You will not bother Santa or me again about what happens in our mentoring period." I see Valentine's cheeks start to burn and for a second, I actually think she might hit me.

"Arbor Day," she finally says. "Welcome to Holiday High. Be careful to take care of yourself. " With that, Valentine leaves my room. After she's gone, I take a deep breath. I gather my things and head to Spring's room. Being alone is dangerous here.

"SHE SAID WHAT??" Columbus is instantly angry. We are sitting in Spring's room and I'm recapping to them the encounter with Valentine. Watching Columbus being so angry in Spring's pastel room is truly a sight to see. "I can't believe it. Who does she think she is? She never would have pulled that if I were there." Spring sits silently, watching Columbus pace around.

Shadow's eyes are closed and she seems to be trying to figure all this out.

"If Fairy has told you not to say anything about mentoring, then there is nothing you can do, Arbor." Spring advises. "Valentine is just used to having her way. Columbus was right. If you had been with us, she would never have attempted something like that." I sit and think about the interaction with Valentine. In some ways, I'm very proud of the fact that I kept the contents of the mentoring group silent, but maybe treating her the way Frost treats us wasn't the answer, either. I explain this to the girls.

"You did the right thing," Shadow says, opening her eyes. "You have to understand that Valentine will only continue to mess with you if you give into her. I've spent my entire life around the Majors. My parents have faced numerous attempts to have our status removed as a Major Holiday. They taught me all along that no holiday is better than another and only by working together will our holidays truly be the strongest. Every year, they are afraid that one of the Holiday Council is going to use their Revoking on me."

"Revoking?" I ask. Shadow sighs and continues on. "Each year after the Confirmation, any member of the Holiday Council can revoke a holiday's status. For me, that would be revoking our status as a Major. I would then be considered a Minor and, therefore, have to be part of the Confirmation each year. Not to mention that my parents would lose their status and their vote on who the head of the Holiday Council would be. "

'For us Minors," Spring explains. "It means that we're no longer deemed worthy and can no longer attend Holiday High." "So we can go throughout this entire year, work super hard, present at the Confirmation and then any of the seven members of the Council can revoke us?" I say, bewildered.

"If a revoking is used, then that holiday cannot use a revoking for another 25 years," Shadow says. "That's in place to prevent any one holiday from filling the council with like-minded people.

There hasn't been a revoking for over 100 years. No one wants to risk it. "If that was meant to make me feel better, it didn't. Not with what Fairy is asking of Santa and myself. I feel more than ever like a target is on my back.

"Did you really talk to her like you were Frost?" Columbus asks with a gleam in her eye. I laugh. "I sure did." "Tell me everything," she says, sitting down in front of me. "I would have loved to have seen her face."

The rest of the afternoon is relaxing. I don't risk going back to my room, so I actually make all the girls happy by watching movies with them. I'm also relieved to know that on the weekends, we're allowed to have our meals upstairs. Columbus and Spring go get our food, so I don't even have to worry about facing Valentine. But tonight is the back-to-school bonfire and there will be no getting out of seeing her there. Spring comes up with the idea of putting red and green ribbons in our hair. "That will show her we're together," she says, way too excited about ribbons. "Yeah, it will," says Columbus. "And if she messes with you again...well, she better not mess with you again." I can't help but smile. Maybe I've finally found friends.

We made our way out to the back of Holiday High. It was just getting dark and we could see the wooden structure that will the bonfire.

It's tall and impressive. Slightly leaning to the right, the wood was over ten feet tall. We seem to be some of the last students to arrive and most are already standing around waiting for the fun to begin. As we're approaching, Spring is talking nonstop about the night ahead. I'm mostly tuning her out until I hear my name. "And Arbor, you're going to *LOVE* the food. Muffin has created this S'more's muffin that's the greatest thing. Get this; you can still put it on a stick!" I'm starting to admire Spring for all the positivity that she brings to my life. If I had my way or if I was home, I would be sitting alone somewhere. Doing anything on a Saturday is totally foreign to me. I smile, thinking about the fact my parents are probably at home playing games like they do every Saturday night.

"ATTENTION!!" A loud voice booms and we all stop mingling. Coach Bunyan has perched himself on a platform holding a large torch. "Are you guys ready for fire?" Coach yells with a scary look in his eyes. This guy should not be trusted with a giant torch. The others seem to know this ritual and they respond back to Coach with a loud "YES!" I get caught up in the excitement that seems to be building as Coach marches around the platform chanting, " FIRE! FIRE! FIRE!" Remember, this is a seven-foot-tall man in tight sweatpants. I see Fairy is laughing, so I feel a little safer that he's not going to burn the forest down. That isn't something that my holiday would deem worthy.

Finally, when the excitement is at a fever pitch, Bunyan lifts the torch above his head and releases it onto the wooden structure. The flame bursts up instantly. The WHOOSH of the heat almost knocks me down. The orange beast reaches high in the sky and everyone cheers.

How exactly did I get here? Standing with other girls, with ribbons in my hair, and yelling at a school function. I, Arbor Day, don't even recognize myself anymore. Before I knew, everyone is clapping their hands and chanting, "SPIRIT! SPIRIT! SPIRIT! WE ARE THE HOLIDAY SPIRIT!" The chant goes on for a bit, whipping everyone into a frenzy. I find myself laughing and chanting like the others. Not sure how this is supposed to get me excited about being back at school, but I'm trying my best. After the chanting calms down, I notice some students climbing on top of the platform. Santa, Valentine, Pres, and Flag are above us. "Who is ready for a great year?" Pres says to us. We cheer and a big smile breaks across his face. He puts his hands up to try and quiet us down. "I would like to personally invite you to the back-to-school bonfire. On behalf of your student senate, I want to assure you that we're going to make this the best year ever. "I just love how Pres speaks. So formal. He truly looks in his element when addressing a crowd. "If anyone here ever needs anything, you can come to me. I want you to think of the senate as your voice. If you can't find me, then you can always go to my brand new vice president, FLAG!" With that, the crowd starts to erupt again.

My girls and I started chanting, "FLAG! FLAG! FLAG!" He looks like he's on top of the world. I see that he's decked out in his usual HH gear, but this time, he has gone the extra mile and painted his face red and green. He steps up to the front of the platform and yells, "GO SPIRIT!" This starts the craziness all over again and I can't help but smile. Good for Flag.

Valentine is next. She also calms the crowd down as she begins to address us. "Guys," she starts. "As the head of your party committee, I assure you that this year's Spring formal is going to be one for the ages. We are going all out this year, and you're going to remember it forever." The crowd cheers again. My first reaction isn't to cheer but to question whether or not I want to attend a dance put on by Valentine. "Now I want you to give it up for my boyfriend and our school captain, SANTA!" This time I have trouble cheering along with the rest of the students.

Santa actually looks uncomfortable with all the attention as he makes his way up to speak. Knowing him better now, I see that even despite all the acclaim, he really is just someone who wants to make everyone happy. His smile is genuine here and I know that he loves the fact that there is no fighting right now. At this moment, we're all just students. We are young, energetic and ready to take on the school year. We are not Minors or Majors. We aren't concerned with the labels. Right now, we're all deemed worthy and I know that this is what Santa wants. If I could bottle this moment up, I would. For the first time since mentoring began, I feel a connection to him. All these people are excited to see him and hear him speak, but only I get to meet with him in that setting to really get to know him more. I make a mental note to tell him that on Monday. That I'm honored to be in this fight with him.

"I want us to remember one thing this year," Santa says. The crowd is instantly hushed. I smile and wonder if Santa even knows the power and respect he yields. "I want us to remember that we're all holidays! Not Minors. Not Majors. We are the Holiday High Spirit! Let's join together and make this the best year EVER!" With that speech, the crowd goes nuts. I cheer louder than anyone. I can't believe he just said that. I look over again at Fairy and she meets my eyes. She winks at me and starts cheering, too. I'm happy at this moment. I'm still stunned that I feel this happy at a place I dreaded for months. I pull my eyes away from Fairy when I notice Frost behind her. He isn't cheering. In fact, it looks like he thinks what Santa said is the worst possible thing ever. He suddenly locks onto my eyes. Even from here, I can feel the chill. I turn my gaze away and start cheering again. For tonight, I can put Frost out of my mind.

After the speeches, we're gathered around the fire to roast our Muffins. That in itself was amazing. Spring told the truth and you can actually cook them on a stick. I began watching everyone around the fire. My girls are enjoying themselves tremendously.

Along with Flag and Pres, they were laughing up a storm, trying to watch Columbus eat the muffin. She's getting chocolate all over her face. She looks like she has a mustache. "My dad always wanted a boy!" she cries with tears rolling down her face.

"Fun night, isn't it?" I turn, and there is Patrick. He is smiling and has two drinks in his hands. "This is apple cider," he says, offering me a cup.

I give him a questionable look, but take the drink anyway. I take a sip. Man, this is good. "So, you have been avoiding me?" Patrick asks. I smile and kind of shrug my shoulders. I'm not going to admit to anything. But of course I've been avoiding him. I still haven't figured that night out. It confuses me so much when I think back to sitting in the cafeteria. I've never opened up to a guy like that before. Plus, he hasn't sat with us since that first morning, so who is to say he thought it was anything special? So now this is just awkward. So what do I do when things are awkward? I make it more awkward.

"Are you here to take me on another date?" That was apparently not what Patrick thought I was going to say. He chokes up on his drink and starts to cough. I laugh and wait for him to start breathing again. If I'm being honest, there hasn't been a night since that I haven't been tempted to go back to the study lounge. But nerves keep me in my room.

"It may not be a date, but I've been waiting for you to come back to the study lounge," Patrick says. The uncomfortable turning in my stomach returns. I find it hard to believe Patrick has been sitting in the Study Lounge each night, waiting for me to come down. If he only knew.

My mind starts to go in many different directions. Part of me is thrilled to be talking to Patrick again after a week of trying my hardest not to speak to him. Other thoughts invade my mind, making me feel like every single person is watching us right now. When, in actuality, it looks like no one is noticing us.

"If you have been waiting for me each night, then why didn't you say something?" I asked. "You sat with us that next morning and then nothing. You can't possibly expect me to believe that you're serious." Even I'm taken aback by my hostile tone. But if Patrick is hurt, he doesn't show it. Instead, he takes my hand and leads me away from the crowd. This time, when he takes my hand, I'm not as shocked. In fact, it feels nice. It feels special. Columbus shoots me a look, and I wave her off.

"Arbor," Patrick says, stopping us a few feet away from the festivities. "I *have* been wanting to talk to you since that night. You seemed so uncomfortable when I sat at your table for breakfast that I didn't want to embarrass you any further. I kept thinking that you would surely come back to the study lounge and we could talk. But you never did. Why is that?" I take a long look at Patrick. I see those deep green eyes. I notice his shamrock necklace isn't visible tonight. I want to believe him. He seems sincere. Did he really not sit with us again because of the way I was acting?

"I don't open up to people that often," I explain to him. I notice the sparks flying off the bonfire in the background. It looks like fireflies are circling around Patrick's head. "I've been nervous about being around you ever since then. Nervous that the time spent with you wasn't really that meaningful. That you were just being nice to me since I'm the new holiday. I don't want to expect more openness from you if it was just good manners on your part." At this junction in time, I really do wish I was anywhere else but Holiday High. Before this week, I didn't have these problems. I close my eyes and wait for his response. Before he can speak, I hear a commotion coming from the bonfire area. I hear chanting and a group of students marching towards the fire. They seem to be holding up a large doll-like figure. We stand there for a bit, watching what is going on.

"What is this?" I ask Patrick.

"I have no clue. Looks like Valentine is up to something," he replies back.

We make our way back to the fringe of the group and sure enough, Valentine, April, and some of the other Majors are marching. They seem to be chanting, "MAJORS! MAJORS! MAJORS!" We are now back standing by the girls and Spring grabs my hand. As they get closer, I start to make out the wooden figure they have made. It looks like a stick body with long brown straw-like hair. It's wearing old green and red clothes that resemble a school uniform.

Suddenly, Patrick looks at me. "Hey, why don't we head back to the school? I'm getting pretty tired." That's strange. It's barely after 9 P.M. "That sounds like a great idea, Patrick," Spring says. At this point, the marching students have reached the bonfire and are preparing for some sort of action. Patrick and Spring are both trying to turn me away and head back. I'm curious to see what is going on.

Valentine is again on the platform, overlooking the students. April hands her the figure and Valentine addresses the crowd. I pull away from Spring and Patrick. I make my way up to the rest of the students. Pushing my way past Columbus and I stand there with Shadow. Now that I'm closer, I see the figure is wearing a red cloth around her neck tied in a bow. I put my hand to my mouth. The figure is me. Shadow turns to me and tries to move me away. But I can't move. I'm too shocked. Valentine yells to the crowd; holding up the figure, she proclaims, "Welcome to Holiday High!" She then tosses the figure in the fire and her group of Majors starts to cheer.

At this point, my world turns into slow motion. This happens to me whenever I'm in shock. I look around and everyone is talking and moving at a lethargic speed. My friends are trying to talk to me. Patrick is trying to get my attention. I see Santa standing by the platform, looking confused. All I can really see is Valentine staring me down, her words ringing in my ears. "Welcome to Holiday High."

The world comes back to me in rapid swoosh. I'm breathing heavily and everyone is now talking to me all at once. I pull away from them all. I stumble out of the group and take off for the school. I was never meant to be here.

CHAPTER TEN

I turned into the school and up to the girl's side. The only
person I see is Sandman, who I almost knock down, turning
the stairs that lead up to the third floor.

"Miss Arbor Day, where are you going? Are you okay?
Shouldn't you be at the bonfire?" he yells up at me. His fast speech
matching my frantic speed up the steps. I tear down the hallway
and throw open my door. I sit down against the door and just try
to calm my breathing. *I will not cry. I can't cry.* I don't want to give
that girl and the other Majors the joy of knowing that they have
gotten to me that deeply. I sit and stare around the room. For the
first time since I've been here, its magic does not work. It looks
dark. Cold. The cozy feeling I've enjoyed for the past week isn't
present. I long for my room back home. The green and brown
earthy tones of my walls. My canopy bed. Even all my dolls that are
still residing around my room.

The only thing I can do right now is do the one thing that I
can always rely on. I raise myself up, slipping off my shoes. I walk
up the two steps and lie down in the bed. Before I can even close
my eyes, I hear Spring knocking on the door. I hear her and other

girls calling for me, but I ignore them. Covering my head with my pillow, I lay there until they go away. I don't belong here.

That's what is running through my mind as I drift off. I wake up and it's still dark outside. It takes a minute for the memories of the bonfire to rush back to me. I'm forced to relive the moment again as I lay there on the bed. I look at the clock and groan—3 A.M. I make my way up off the bed. I change out of my smoke-soaked clothes and change into fresh sleepwear. I rub my eyes and open the door to go to the bathroom. I'm stopped right away as Spring is curled up in front of my door. She's lying there covered by a blanket, her head resting on a pillow.

For some reason, this finally sets me off. I sit down beside her and start crying. Why am I even here? I hate crying and it makes me so angry. I don't think I have what it takes for this battle between Minors and Majors. This isn't my fight. My life was fine. My life was calm.

Spring starts to stir and then slowly opens her eyes. "Arbor!" She says, sitting straight up. Her hair is standing up, and she has the creases on her face from the pillow. Before I can say a word, she's hugging me tight, which makes me cry even harder. "I'm so sorry," she repeats to me over and over. She lets me go and looks me in the eye. I see that she has joined me in the crying.

"Listen, you can't let them get to you. Valentine and the others are just..." She pauses. "Well, they are mean and stupid!" With that we both start laughing. Both crying from laughter and tears. She helps me up and we make our way to the bathroom where I clean up a bit.

We make it back to my room and I collapse on my chair. Spring sits on the floor in front of me. "We aren't going to let them treat you this way," she says, looking up at me. Even though Spring is a good six inches shorter than me, I can't help but smile. She has such a motherly instinct about her. "Columbus is already planning her revenge. She wants to sneak into Valentine's room and shave her curly hair off!" I start laughing again, but I would really love to see a bald Valentine.

"I don't want to be here anymore," I confess to Spring. I tell her about the fight to come here, the first night with Patrick, and the talk I had with him earlier tonight. It feels good to open up to Spring. The more I confide in her, the more I feel some of the humiliation wash off me. "I really want to think Patrick is sincere," I tell her. "But after tonight, I don't think I can trust any of the Majors again. Well, except Shadow." Spring gets a serious look on her face. It's so cute the way she straightens her back when she's about to say something serious.

"Patrick is different this year," she replies. "While he wasn't as bad as Valentine and some of the others, he still only hung out with other Majors. This year, I've noticed that he seems to be distant from them. Mostly just being alone. Like he's stuck between the two." It makes sense what she says. While he does sit with the Big Four at their table, he always seems off to the side, not really interacting. It starts to dawn on me how little I know about this school. How am I supposed to have figured this all out in a week? Perhaps some of the problem has been me, thinking I had to know everything right now. To be in control.

"And how will I face Santa in mentoring on Monday?" I ask, burying my head in my hands. "I don't think that's going to be an issue," Spring says. I look up questionably.

"I took off right after you, but Columbus and Shadow hung around..." She goes on, "Well, Shadow stayed because she had to make sure Columbus didn't cause Valentine bodily harm. They told me that Santa and Valentine got into a big argument. No one could hear them as he had pulled her away from the fire. But Shadow said that in all the time she has known Santa, she has never seen him this angry. His face was as red as Rudolph's nose. He stormed off, leaving Valentine there by herself. So yeah, I don't think he was too happy with what happened."

We stay up a bit longer. Spring tells me over and over again that tomorrow, we're going to show a united front. That we girls are going to march into breakfast tomorrow morning and show the Majors that they didn't get to us. She makes me swear over and over again that I won't leave Holiday High. "I think you're exactly what this school needs," she tells me. We both finally start to yawn and give in to sleep. Spring insists on staying with me tonight.

"It's not like I'm going to leave school tonight," I tell her, but she doesn't listen and even spends extra time tucking me in my bed. She makes a little space on the floor and settles in to sleep. A few minutes go by. "Thank you, Spring," I say quietly. She doesn't answer. I look down and she's already sleeping.

The next morning, I'm jolted awake to the all-familiar banging on my door. I groan and open my eyes. I see Spring jump up and open the door. Columbus and Shadow make their way in. Columbus crosses straight over to me, hovers above me, and places her hands on her hips. "Do you want me to go punch Valentine right in the face?" She says with authority. "I'm serious. Say the word and I will gladly knock that girl out." I'm tempted for a second to say yes. What a sight it would be to see Columbus march down the hall, barge into Valentine's room, and punch her right in the face. But sadly, I think that would not solve anything.

"No, thank you," I say, grinning up at her. She collapses on the bed beside me. "You also can't leave," she says to me. "I agree," Shadow says, joining us on the bed. Spring hops up and all four of us are lying on my now too small bed. "Valentine has been known to pull some stunts, but nothing like that," Shadow explains. "You must have really done something to really get to her and whatever that is I love it and want more of it."

"Right on, sister," Columbus says, as all four of us laugh at Columbus's attempt at sisterhood. "What am I going to do?" I sigh. "I don't want this. Is it possible to just stay here in my room? Take all my classes in here?" I start to dream about this life. I can live like a squirrel in a tree. I can get a stash of food and never have to leave. I only have to figure out the bathing and the going to the bathroom part. Shadow sits up and then crawls over all four of us to get out of the bed. She stands up, straightens out her dress, and looks us over.

'The question is," she starts. "What are we going to do about it? I'm locked in now and ready to take this war to them. I'm a Major. I may be the only Major that cares that the differences between the two holidays are growing. But this has to stop." I'm in shock. Here is another Major, one besides Patrick and Santa, that's saying the same thing. That change needs to happen. Also, here is another ally besides Santa and Fairy for me to lean on. "And Arbor, it starts this morning. We are going to go into breakfast united, and they will not dare to cross us." With that, Spring jumps over us and tackle hugs Shadow. "Oh, Shadow, you old softy!" Spring says. Columbus jumps up and joins them. They all look at me. I smile and join them. How exactly did I end up here?

We all get ready to head downstairs. Each of the girls wear a red ribbon around their neck to show their support for me. Spring and Shadow look wonderful with it on. Columbus tries her best but it just doesn't fit with her sporty style. Still, she refuses to take it off. We don't see anyone else as we make our way down the stairs. "We must be running late," Spring says.

We march our way down the hall arm in arm. I start to hesitate the closer we get to the dining hall. The girls won't let me go and even drag me the rest of the way. We stop right before we enter. They all look at me. "Are we really going to do this?" I ask. "You know we can just go back upstairs. We can stream movies, do our hair, paint our nails."

"First," says Columbus, "No to all of that, and second, we're here with you." She starts hopping up and down and shaking her hands. "Now come on, team! Let's get in there and show them what we're made of. "We all laugh and open the door. I dread what the response is going to be.

But the dining hall is empty. No one. Only Muffin is behind the counter, placing muffins into a pyramid shape. We just stand there and look at each other. We bust into fits of laughter. What a waste of an entrance! Still laughing, we say good morning to Muffin and head to our table. French toast muffins. It feels like he has injected each one with syrup and sugar. For a brief moment we enjoy the place to ourselves. We make a pact that when Valentine shows up, we won't even acknowledge her.

Others finally start to trickle in. Some of them are part of her crew from last night, but we pay them no mind. I do see some glances our way, but I'm trying my hardest to stay strong. Pres, Fall and Flag finally arrive. Flag almost knocks me out of my chair with the biggest hug. "You are still here, Arbor!" he says. I smile and hug him back. Fall even stays awake long enough to give me the OK signal. I nod at him and he lays his head down. Strangely, I'm honored by that. Pres joins us and is looking all serious.

"Arbor," he says, setting his tray down. "Last night isn't what Holiday High is all about it. You say the word and I will make this a senate issue. I won't rest until she's punished." I can't help but laugh. I feel bad, but he's so adorable with all his formality. He looks hurt at first, but then he cracks up with the rest of us. For the next few minutes, I forget all about last night. We are just enjoying our Sunday. Flag is entertaining us with a story about how he was able to fit seven muffins on his stick last night when Valentine and April make their appearance. By the look of her you would have thought she was the one humiliated the night before.

Her hair is pulled back with a strap and her normally made-up face is nowhere to be seen. She's decked out in HH sweats and she looks like she had a rough night. My eyes follow her as she makes her way through the line and to her table. She sits down and motions April to go and get her a milk. She looks at me and I can see how red her eyes are from here. It may be from lack of sleep, from crying, or it could be her blood boiling since the look she's sending to me is death. She's joined by three of the Big Four.

The mismatched dressed Bunny (Easter), the girl beside him dressed today like an amine' creature (That's Hallow. She's really into Theater), and finally, the big guy Turkey (Thanksgiving). They all seem scared of her at this moment. She finally looks away from me. I survey the other table in the dining hall. That's where the rest of the Minors sit, plus Fourth and Pop. J.J. is really the one that I've gotten to know. For the first time, it strikes me that there are more Minors than Majors.

Maybe that's why they fear us? I make a mental note to ask Fairy about the rest of the holidays. I found it important to know about all the holidays. I don't have time to think about this as Santa and Patrick enter.

They both make their way through the line, grab their milk, and walk straight to our table. The rest of the hall watches as they grab chairs and sit with us. At this moment, I don't even dare look at Valentine. The boys start to eat and don't even look at their normal table. It takes the rest of the students some time to recover from this event. It takes our table even longer. This time, it's Shadow who moves us along.

"Well," she says. "This is something new." Pres elbows Fall awake and points. He looks at Santa and Patrick. "Hey guys," he says, laying his head back down. Flag just keeps looking back and forth between Patrick and Santa, a big grin on his face.

"Good morning," I say. I try to make it sound casual like this is just another normal day. "Good morning, Arbor," Patrick replies. "It's good to see you're still here." He smiles at me and I think back to last night when we were holding hands. "Yes, it's very good," Santa adds. "I nearly broke the third-floor rule last night. I wasn't about to let you leave." He, too, smiles at me. This Santa seems a little different. More relaxed, more resolved. "But of course," he continues,. "I fear the Sandman too much." He starts to laugh and the rest of us relax a little. The boys finish eating and then Santa looks at us.

"Okay, guys," he starts. "Patrick and I were up all night talking and some things are going to change. For starters, Valentine and I are on a break. What she and the rest of her crew did last night was beyond repulsive. She's not the girl I first started dating and from this point on, I don't know if she ever will be again." We all look at him with the same look of disbelief. "Second," he continues, "we, and I mean everyone at this table, are now equals. We are going to show everyone at this school what it means to work together as holidays." I know I'm shocked, so I can imagine that everyone else is, too. The words that Santa is speaking right now are powerful and motivating.

"All of us together." With that, Santa finishes. He looks around the table, taking his time to let each of us know he's serious. His eyes land on Fall and he laughs. "Will he be okay with all of this?" he asks. "Most definitely," answers Spring.

"This is how we're going to do it," Patrick speaks up. He has the entire attention of the table now. Well, except for Fall. We sit there in anticipation, waiting for the plan that Patrick is about to lay out before us. Last night, as I was lying in bed contemplating a way to exile myself from the school, I had no way of knowing that two of the Majors were also contemplating. Patrick slowly looks around the table. He readies himself and starts to speak.

"Together. That's the only way this works." He pauses and lets that sink in. I wonder back to what Spring told me last night about Patrick being different this year. I wonder if he would have been ready for this a year prior. I'm suddenly curious about what happened during that family trip this summer.

"Sitting at this table are students with the potential to turn this system upside down. We are all going to use our unique and distinct talents. If we all, myself included, strive to be the best version of ourselves and NEVER settle for the way things have always been done, then the archaic ways of doing things won't last."

"Patrick is right. We talked about this all night. Everyone here brings something valuable to the table, pun intended," Santa says, smiling.

'Starting with you, Flag," Santa says, turning to the curly-headed boy. Flag's eyes bug out of his head. "Santa knows my name," he whispers.

"You're right. I do. I also know if you're naughty or nice, but that's for a different time." He laughs and I see Flag is in awe. "Flag, you have the brains we need. But I also know you're kind of sneaky, too." If Flag's face was a mile wide, it still wouldn't be able to hold his smile. "No one is smarter than you, so I want you to learn. Learn all you can this year. Pour yourself into your history lessons. See if you can find in our past where things turned for the worse. Let's learn from the mistakes."

You can see Flag sit up straighter, his shoulders back and chest swelling with pride. I have no doubt he's going to do all he can to help us.

"Pres," Patrick starts in again. "No one in this school is trusted more by the faculty than you. That's why they chose you as the senate leader. We need someone on our behalf who can speak to them—someone who knows how to present in a professional and elite way. That's you. Or we can send Shadow to do it." The whole table laughs at this, including Shadow. Pres has his Presidential face on now, serious look, deep in thought. He gives both Santa and Patrick a short nod. I know he's in.

"Actually, Shadow is important," Patrick continues. "Since no one ever really expects you to talk that much, they rarely remember that you're in the room." I see Shadow's eyes gleam at this. I see the wheels starting to turn.

"So I just keep quiet and listen. Right?" Shadow asks.

"Exactly," Patrick says. "Let them speak. Majors love to talk about themselves."

"Done," Shadow says, not even hesitating. I love this girl.

"Now, you two." Santa turns to Spring and Columbus. "Spring, everyone knows you're the mom here." Spring blushes but smiles. "So I want you to do what Mom's do best. Encourage us. This is going to be a long, hard, intense, dangerous road. We are going to want to quit. To give up. But you can't let us."

"I won't," Spring replies. "I agree with everything. The people here are phenomenal. We will do this."

"Now that's what I'm looking for, Mom," Santa says. He then turns to address Columbus, who has been strangely quiet and is now shifting uncomfortably in her seat.

"We need a Coach," Santa offers. "We need that person that's going put us in our place. We need that person that's going to be mean. We need," Santa pauses. "Well, we need you, Columbus. No one is more intense. We need that intensity in every single one of us." A small smile breaks across Columbus' face.

"You know I'm going to push you hard, Santa," she says to him.

"I'm betting on it," he replies.

"If I do this, I don't want coal in my stocking," she laughs.

"Never," Santa says. "Nothing but rainbows and ponies for you."

"Never," Columbus says.

"What about Fall?" Flag asks. Poor Fall, still asleep.

"Fall is the best athlete we have. I think he's even better than me," Santa says. "I'm sure we will need him at some point."

"This is amazing," I speak up. "But I don't really know what I can offer. I just got here. All of you know how this place works. I have no clue how to handle any of this. You all saw what happened last night." I look at all the others at the table. What a great bunch of people. There is no way I can be a part of this. They need someone better, someone smarter, and someone not me.

"The fact that you have only been here a week is your biggest asset," Patrick says.

I'm waiting for the laugh to come. He has to be joking. I look at Santa. He, too, is wearing a look of seriousness.

"You are coming into this school with a fresh set of eyes. Actually into this world with those fresh eyes. Shadow, Santa, and I've been around Holiday High and the council all our lives. But you haven't. You can see what is messed up better than us."

"Plus, you have a knack for speaking honestly," Santa says. "We need that. Unfiltered and untainted." I look at Spring and she's nodding at me.

"They are right," she says.

"You can do it," Columbus adds. I smile and look around at the others. They all look the same. Like they truly believe in me and trust me.

"Suck it up, Arbor," Shadow says. "You're in it with us now."

CHAPTER ELEVEN

The next two months go by in a flash. When I'm not bogged down with schoolwork, I'm busy with Mentoring. Fairy loved my idea of learning as much I could about the other holidays. So on top of my normal workload, I'm constantly reading. Flag has been a lifesaver. He not only reads fast, but seems to remember everything he reads. Thankfully for me, he never gets tired of having me quiz him. Santa and Patrick were right about him. He is a pure genius.

I also have Spring and Columbus, too. We have all been receiving handwritten notes from Spring each week. These are not the two or three sentences of generic words. No. When you get a note from Spring, it's at least five pages, front and back, detailing specific ways that she has seen us shine. Only Spring can write so wonderfully about an answer I gave in Time's history class.

On the other hand, Columbus is quick to get on me when I start being my mopey, whiny, want-to-leave-it-all self, which is about once a day. "Stop that whining, Ms. Whiny Pants!" She will yell at me. "Things are not going to get better. Things will not get easier with you whining." When she switches into "coach mode," it always makes me laugh. Despite that laughter, I know she's right.

I've dedicated myself to this. I'm in it 100%. But still, that doesn't stop me from putting on the whiny pants act at least some of the time.

The biggest change has been from Santa. Not only are Valentine and he still not dating, but he has taken on a whole new level of engagement. He makes an effort each week to talk to every Minor holiday. The effect this had was instant. He is treating everyone as if they are a vital part of this school. People are embracing it and passing it on to other holidays. Just last week, Mem (Memorial Day) caught the wrath of Valentine in one of Reaper's art lessons. Mem and Shadow switched tracks so Shadow could engage in her "spy mode," as she calls it. Santa stepped in right away and kept the shy girl away from Valentine.

Mem is the cutest thing you have seen. She's skinny and frail and always dressed in a red or green sweater. Being so cold, she asked Reaper to turn up the heat, and Valentine took personal offense to this, telling Mem that she doesn't dictate the temperature.

I've been spending almost every night in the Study Lounge with Patrick. Most of it is spent actually studying and working on our projects. I'm amazed at how smart he is. People don't realize how much work he puts into keeping his grades perfect. I often leave before midnight, but he's always still going. Always. I asked him once when he leaves, and he just said, "When I'm done."

There are times when he would relax and not be so stressed about the work. He would test out new recipes on me. Some are good, like jelly-filled peanut butter muffins, and some are not so good. Beef stew muffins were not his best idea. Or when he tells about his life growing up. He had me in tears telling me about the last time his father tried to spank him.

"I knew it was coming, so I put on six pairs of sweats and like three pairs of underwear. I started acting like it was hurting, but I'm a terrible actor. My father realized soon that it wasn't hurting me."

Patrick is very patient with me. I've made an effort to open up. I tell him about my job working with kids at the park. I also share about our tradition of watching Christmas movies on Christmas Eve and Christmas Day at our house. He finds it interesting that my mom always puts a dash of sugar in our mac and cheese. "I think that would be disgusting!' he exclaims.

"Oh, but it's not!" I say. "It adds just a little bit of sweetness to it. Soooooooo good."

One day at dinner, Santa announces. "Everyone be in the Study Lounge at 11 tonight. It's usually clear then, right?" He asks, looking at Patrick.

"Sure is," he replies.

"Great. See you guys then."

That night, I make my way down to the lounge with the girls. When we get there, the boys are already there. We make our way over to the couches and chairs. Fall curls up in the biggest one. He lays his head down but stays awake. I silently start a clock in my head. Let's see how long until he's out. Santa and Patrick stand before us. Everyone seems on edge. This is more serious than I thought it would be.

"The Holiday Battle is next week," Santa begins. "Arbor, the Holiday Battle is a three-part yearly competition pitting two teams of holidays against each other. The winning team gets the Holiday Cup and bragging rights for the next year. "

"We also get to pick the theme for the Spring Formal," Patrick adds. "Exactly," continues Santa. "Understand this: The Spring Formal is Valentine's baby and she will do anything to protect her baby."

"I'm confused," I say. "Didn't Valentine already announce at the bonfire that the Spring Formal is already set? She said, and I quote, it's going to be the best thing ever, or out of this world or blow our minds. Something like that?"

"She did," Santa answers me. "She said it because her team

never loses. In the past, the teams have always been Majors vs. Minors. But not this year. This year, we shake things up.

Turkey has been asked to be one of the team Captains. Pres is the other one. " We all look at Pres, who smiles and nods.

"I love it," Shadow says. "Maybe this year I won't be stuck with only Majors."

"So let me get this right," I say. "Three competitions. Two teams. One winner?"

"Yes," Patrick and Santa say together.

"Ok, so what are these three competitions?" I ask.

"Physical, Mental, and Surprise," Pres says. "Last year, it was an obstacle course, science experiment, and then fashion. You never really know what you're going to get until it starts. Sometimes we don't even get to the surprise competition as the Majors win the first two.

I think of all the different things that they could name for a competition—archery, water skiing, dog grooming. Maybe I will get lucky and it will be tree trimming. "So the plan is that we get this group on the same team," Santa says.

"How are the teams selected?" I ask. I really don't like being the one person not knowing. "It's a draft!" says a very excited Columbus. "Each captain takes turns picking who they want on their team. It's an unwritten rule that Majors pick Majors. Minors pick Minors."

"Which is why I'm never asked to be a Captain," Shadow interjects. "I would take their precious unwritten rule and flush it."

"He is always the first pick," Santa continues. "The rules state that the previous year's loser gets first pick. So if Pres takes me, it's going to send shock waves. After that, there is no telling what will happen, but I'd bet all the cookies my father gets on Christmas Eve that Valentine will make sure Turkey picks her first. She's that vain. It means that much to her."

"There are twenty-two students this year and only nine of us," Flag says. "We will have two others on our teams."

"I have an idea," Spring pipes up. We all look and she smiles big. "Let's take J.J. She's super smart and will be so excited to be playing. She won't have the history of losing. "Sounds awesome," Santa says. "Everyone good with J.J.?" We all nod.

"So that's ten," Says Patrick. "Who is our number eleven?"

"I know who." We all look and Fall is still awake. "We need April."

CHAPTER TWELVE

What did you just say?" Shadow looks stunned. We all do. April? Valentine's best friend? We all stare at Fall. He stares back at us. His usually sleepy face is alert and focused.

"Are you sleep-talking?" Columbus asks. "No," He replies. "I'm wide awake."

Well, this is a twist, I think. There are so many other better options for our team. Mem would be good. Fourth would be good as long as we can keep him calm. But April? I can't imagine how she's going to be beneficial to us.

"Ok, Fall," Santa says. "Why April?" Fall looks around at us. I don't think I've heard Fall say more than five words at a time. Besides class, I don't even think I've seen him awake for five minutes at a time. Spring is usually the sibling that's one for speeches.

"Think about it, guys," Fall begins. "She's the perfect asset. If we choose her during the draft, Valentine is going to be livid. No athlete, performer, speaker, or anyone—does their best when mad. Anger is the greatest distraction. Especially if it's a blindside and comes out of nowhere. Plus, April will know all of Valentine's plans and secrets. It's perfect."

We all look at each other. Fall looks so certain. Could he be right? What Fall is saying makes sense, but I'm not sure I trust April. Anyone who is that close to Valentine has to have some of her awfulness in them.

"How do you know she won't just try to sabotage us?" I ask. The others nod in agreement; they must have been thinking the same thing. April could use this as a chance to cause us even more damage than if we just left her with Valentine.

'She won't." This time, it's Spring speaking up. "If she was to sabotage our team, causing us to lose the Holiday Cup, then that would look terrible in the eyes of the Council. Remember, she's a Major. She doesn't have to go through the Confirmation like the rest of us. No amount of allegiance to Valentine is more important than her holiday being bumped down to Minor status. I think Fall is right; let's draft her." A big smile breaks out on Fall's face.

"It makes sense," Pres pipes in. "Next to drafting Valentine herself, this fits the keep-your-enemies-closer the best." "Alright," Patrick says. "Fall says we should take April. Spring says April won't sabotage us, and I think she's right. We all good with this? Taking J.J. and April as the other two members of our team?"

I nod right away. I trust anything Spring says. No one looks really happy about it, especially Shadow, but we all nod our agreement.

The next week, as the Battle approaches, we try our best to prepare ourselves for any competition that may come up. We are working hard in P.E., studying extra chapters in our books and brainstorming the draft to try and figure out the right order in which to take everyone. Shadow reports to us that none of the Majors suspect a thing. She says that Turkey is doing nothing but telling everyone how they are going to win easily this year.

"I've never met anyone who fits their name better," she says to us at dinner one night. "He is just struts around acting like the Minors have no chance." The bottom line is that we can study all we want, strategize all we want, and come up with all the plans we can, but numerous things can go wrong, which is probably why I can't sleep and find myself in the study lounge with Patrick.

I'm supposed to be focusing on my upcoming philosophy test in St. Nick's class, but nothing is sinking in. The more I try to focus, the more I just get frustrated. I have no doubt Plato is important and had many things to say, but tonight he's just annoying me. I finally push my notes aside and lay my head flat down on the table. A groan escapes. Patrick laughs, not taking his eyes off his notes. I groan again and lean back in my chair. "This isn't funny, sir," I say to him. "Not all of us have the superhuman ability to be perfect. Can't tomorrow just hurry up and get here?"

"Everything is going to be fine, Arbor," he says, still studying. I find it funny that he can carry on a whole conversation with me without losing focus. What I would give for that ability. As tonight is proving, I can't keep my mind at ease if too much is going on.

"Well, aren't you confident," I say, pouting a little. "Nowhere in that super brain of yours is there a scenario where things aren't fine?" He smiles, finishes writing and takes his glasses off. He looks stressed. I instantly feel bad for getting onto him. I don't have a quarter of the pressure he feels. Again, I start to admire him for what he does and on top of all that he has taken upon himself to help change this school.

"It's not that I don't think something can go wrong," he explains. "But no matter what happens, as long as we break up the Majors and Minors, then it's a victory. We can't control everything that's going to happen, just like we can't control what competitions will be chosen. All we can do is be as prepared as we can. I was talking to Sarge (Veteran's Day) the other day, and he was telling me about the Marine Corps training. You can read all about the training, watch all the training videos, and talk to as many

Marines as possible, but it still won't prepare you. The only thing you can prepare for is that you can't prepare. You have to just expect anything to happen. He is a smart cookie. He is more than guns and prepping for the apocalypse."

I laugh at this. Sarge is different for sure. Tall, broad-shouldered, with a clean crew cut. I didn't even know they had red camouflage or red combat boots until I got here. It doesn't surprise me that it's Patrick that sees beyond the gruffness. "When did you talk to him?" I ask.

"Well, he's in my Track and I realized a few weeks ago that I probably haven't talked to him more than a few times," he says to me. "It's not something I'm proud of. I can't believe that I've gone to school with these other holidays and never even thought to get to know them." There's that look again. The one of pain and shamefulness.

"What exactly happened this summer?" I ask him. He looks at me with a questioning face. "Spring and the others have all mentioned that you're different this year. Gone is the know-it-all who they have known for years." I pause. "So what happened? You went overseas, got a shamrock necklace and now here we are." At this moment, I start to think that I've overstepped my bounds. Sure, we have been spending time together, but that doesn't mean he's ready to bare his soul to me. Especially since my soul is such a hard nut to crack. "Saint Patrick happened," he tells me. Now, it's my turn to give him a questioning look.

"When we went over this summer, we visited Ireland and our family." Right now, Patrick looks tired, which is surprising to me since he never seems to run out of energy.

"The keepers of our holiday in Ireland view things very differently from the way we view it here. Here my father is all concerned about making our holiday one of the biggest. Nothing matters but how many celebrate it, how many parties are thrown, or how many parades are held. It's all about how much money we can bring in and how close we can get to the Big Four. He is obsessed, and I, too, got caught up in that obsession. When I came here, I only thought about how to prove that I was better than everyone else. Even with the culinary arts I wanted to prove to everyone that I was someone who excels in everything. Even something I truly love, like cooking." I sit there in silence. Nothing that he's saying is a surprise to me. The stories about the Major Holidays and all they will do to get bigger are no secret. It's what gives them such an advantage. But to hear it in person, to have a Major freely admit to the greed is fascinating. What is even more fascinating is to hear one of their own children say that it made them want to do the same. Dread comes over me as I realize that the task Fairy put in front of me is daunting.

"So, I spent this summer learning what Saint Patrick was really like. He was unbelievable, Arbor, truly a saint in every way. I've grown up knowing his story, how he was kidnapped by pirates and God leading him back to his home. How when he returned, he dedicated himself to helping others. He wasn't about leprechauns or pots of gold at the end of a rainbow. He really wouldn't want a parade. All he wanted was to help people. That's what my father doesn't like about the shamrock."

He pulls out his necklace and continues. 'This is what Saint Patrick used to explain God to people. To show them love and kindness. That's what the holiday means to my family over there and that's what I'm trying to do this year. The thought of going back to only being concerned about myself, about how everything should be done to benefit the holiday makes me sick. I won't go back to that." He lowers his head, shaking it slowly. I don't know what to do.

Patrick finally looks up and smiles. "That's why I know things will be okay no matter what happens tomorrow, because I'm different now. Because I'm dedicated to making this place change. Every great change that has happened to the world has started with young people. I truly believe we can do something great." I wish I could tell him that his words have worked and I'm suddenly not worried about tomorrow.

But his words have done nothing but make me more anxious. How can a group of high school holidays have enough effect to change the entire system? The scarier question may be, what happens if we don't change it?

Chapter Thirteen

The next morning we all gather in the auditorium. In place of the usual morning assembly we have the selection of teams and also find out what the first competition will be that afternoon. Our normal crew of Minors sits together with Shadow, but Santa and Patrick sit away from us to try not to draw suspicion to our plan. I see Turkey and Valentine laughing up a storm over by the rest of their crew. I really hope this idea works and the draft goes as planned. "You going to calm down?" Shadow asks me when she sees my leg moving nonstop, shaking against her since she is next to me.

"I'm calm," I lie with a smile. "I just hope this goes the way we envision." Finally, it looks like all the students and faculty are here and I watch as Frost makes his way up to the front.

"You will listen to me right now," he says with that cold stare. "Would Pres and Turkey please make their way up-front?" I see Turkey jump up right away and run up the steps to the stage, taking them two at a time, oozing with confidence in this moment. Pres climbs out of our row and makes his way down calmly, as only he can. When he reaches the top of the stage, he makes his way over to Turkey and extends his hand. You hear a snicker go up amongst Valentine and the others. Turkey makes an overdramatic gesture of shaking Pres's hand, laughing the entire time. Once they have shaken, they both move to their podiums. Here it is the moment of truth. Let's just hope this first pick throws everybody for a loop. Before I actually pass out, Frost silences everyone and turns to Pres.

"You will make your first pick now," he says to Pres, who is doing an amazing job looking calm. Perhaps he *is* calm and I'm the only one that's losing it. "You will have two minutes to make your selection. If you have not made your selection within the two-minute limit, then your fellow captain will be allowed to make the next pick. You will not be able to use that pick until the entire selection process is complete." *That would stink*, I say to myself. That means you will be stuck with whoever is left. "You will now begin deliberating on your first pick, Pres."

Here is the moment of truth when all the planning we have done begins. What will the reaction be amongst the fellow students and the faculty? I see Pres slowly check his watch and make a show of shifting around some papers. Shadow starts to chuckle at this and Spring elbows her in the ribs. I check my watch and see that thirty seconds have already passed.

Enough with the show, Pres, and make the pick already. Pres places his hands at the top of the podium and addresses the crowd.

"Ladies and Gentleman of Holiday High," He starts in a most professional manner, making Shadow crack up even more. Spring shoots her a look, which only makes Shadow laugh harder. At least she isn't making any noise. "For the first pick of my team this year I select...," Pres stops and inserts a dramatic pause. "I select Santa. Representing Christmas."

Now I don't know what I was expecting to happen. Would people throw a fit? Would they start yelling? Would everyone start looking at each other in a confused rage, or would the faculty try to reverse the pick? *No way*, I thought. ALL OF THOSE! Instantly Valentine and April start yelling at Pres. Turkey keeps turning back and forth between them and Frost in confusion, all while turning a deep shade of purplish red.

The rest of the students, including us with our best acting ability, are looking at each other, trying to figure out what happened. Only Fourth looks calm. He sits there silently, petting Pop with a serene look on his face. Frost is gripping his podium, turning even more pale than normal. He keeps tapping on the microphone, trying to settle everyone down.

"YOU WILL ALL CEASE TALKING RIGHT NOW!" Frost yells over the crowd. Everyone freezes, even he freezes, at his words. I glance over at the faculty, who look more confused than the students. I make eye contact with Fairy and it's my turn to wink. A big smile spreads across her face.

Frost turns to Pres, and I'm seriously worried that my friend will end up in a block of ice. "You will make your pick again," he informs him. He takes one step towards Pres and points a icy white finger. "You will remember your place this time." Pres looks remarkably calm. At that moment, Fairy rises and addresses the room.

"Everyone, please listen," she says. "Pres's selection stands. The rules state that he may select any student who attends Holiday High, which he has done. The rules also state that no pick may be changed after it's announced. Therefore, the pick stands and Turkey, it seems that you have spent your whole two minutes swiveling your head back and forth like, well, like a Turkey. Your time is now up. Pres your two minutes start now."

Wow. We all start to look at each other and you can see the smile spreading across Santa's face as he's now standing next to Pres. I have to admire Pres. He's still the calmest one in the room. He doesn't look phased by the chaos at all. He looks at Santa, then back out upon us. "I select Patrick, representing St. Patrick's Day." Then, utter mayhem. Frost is shaking his podium, causing icicles to form around it. Turkey's mouth has fallen open, and he looks like he's stunned into a lobotomy. Valentine lets out an audible,

"WHAT?" Everyone is talking non-stop as Patrick makes his way up to stand beside Santa. Shadow has turned almost green from laughing so hard and Fairy is standing up, tapping her wrist, trying to show Turkey his time is already running.

Finally, something clicks in his head and Turkey starts looking in a panic at the rest of the Majors, trying to figure out what to do. Everyone is talking at once and Turkey is cooking under the pressure. "TIME'S UP!" Fairy hollers, silencing everyone. Pres doesn't even hesitate this time. "I select April, representing April Fool's Day." He speaks into the mic. Then, the world comes to an end.

Not really, but close. Frost pushes the podium down, marches down the steps and over to Fairy. She holds up one hand and he stops in his tracks. You can see feel the cold blasting off him. The other two in the Big Four, Hallow and Bunny, are screaming at Santa and Patrick. They are getting so irate that Coach Bunyan has to grab both of them and pull them to the back of the room. It's quite the sight to see Hallow being dragged through the air dressed like a jester today, the bells from her hat ringing loudly. April slowly makes her way up to stand with the rest of the team. She has now replaced Turkey as the most confused person in the room. Valentine walks straight up to Turkey and pushes him to his podium.

"Repeat after me," she orders. "I select Valentine, representing Valentine's Day." Turkey still looks brain-dead but manages to speak in a squeaky voice. "Uh, um," he says, sounding like someone just going through puberty. "I select Valentine, representing Valentine's Day." He manages to get it out before the time is up and his team finally has a member. Frost is slowly making his way back up to the front. He picks up his podium, setting it upright. He speaks in a slow, cold voice. "You will now make your next pick, Pres." He says, not looking anywhere but right at Fairy.

"We select Arbor, representing Arbor Day," Pres announces. While this pick doesn't evoke the uproar of the first three, I still feel daggers being shot at me by the rest of the Majors. I move as quickly as I can to the front, not daring to look at Frost. I take my place next to a still-dazed April. I look forward and try to relax. Valentine slaps Turkey in the back of the head this time. Turkey shakes his face and announces, "I select Hallow, representing Halloween."

"Let me go!" We hear Hallow cry from the back. Coach drops her and she heads up to join Turkey and Valentine. "I select Shadow, representing Groundhog's Day," Pres says.

"Will you stop taking all the Majors!!?" Valentine screams. Shadow makes her way up to the front and goes to the side with Turkey and his team. She then slaps her forehead and laughs before making her way to stand by my side. I've never seen her enjoy something more.

The rest of the draft goes as planned. Turkey takes all the rest of the Majors: Eve, Kris, Fourth, who does not look happy at all, and Bunny. We stick to the plan of selecting Flag, Fall, Spring, Columbus, and J.J.. I feel bad for the others who are left and must be on the other team. When he's forced to, Turkey takes Mardi (Mardi Gras) first of the remaining Minors. It's not a bad pick and Turkey shouldn't be upset. Mardi is wonderful, extremely hyper, but wonderful. We're in big trouble if there is a show-tune competition since Mardi is always belting out songs.

Her blonde curls bounce as she heads to the front. She's followed by the picks of Labor and Sarge. Poor Mem is last selected. She actually looks like a petrified tree as she stands by her team. Frost has calmed a little; we're still surrounded by a cold circle of air but no longer feel like we're floating on an iceberg. He dismisses us to sit with our teams while Coach Bunyan makes his way to the front. "I'm here to announce the first competition," he booms at us. "This event isn't only going to test you physically, but I've been working with Old Man to test you mentally as well. There will be a course set up around the school grounds that you will run as a team. Along the way, you will come across puzzles that you must solve in order to move on. You cannot start the puzzle until all your team members are present." So this is a twist; not only is it physical, but it's mental as well. Looks like we're not the only ones trying to change things up this year. "It's simple," Coach says. "First team that completes the puzzles and makes it back here wins."

Chapter Fourteen

L ater that afternoon we're gathered in the front of the
school decked out in our battle uniforms. Our team has
the privilege of wearing the red uniforms while the others
are sporting the green. As much as I don't like physical activity, at
least I'm going to be comfortable. Being nervous doesn't even
begin to describe how I feel. We are milling around, waiting
anxiously to get things started. I'm having serious doubts if this is
going to work. Our first meeting did not go well. April was not
happy at all about being selected by our team.

She screamed, yelled, fumed, and swore she wouldn't do
anything to help us. Santa kindly reminded her that if she sabo-
taged us during the competition that there was a good chance that
his father would recommend her holiday be bumped back down to
a Minor. That shut her up.

So, here we stand. I huddle next to Shadow to keep from
freezing in the early November air. This is a terrible combination:
being nervous and freezing. At least everyone else looks cold, too,
except for Frost, who would probably be walking around in shorts
if he could. At this moment I'm hoping that the next competition

is going to be inside by the fireplace. It's during this warm dream that I hear Columbus calling us all together.

"Get over here!" She orders. I snap out of it and cold shuffle with Shadow to where Columbus is standing. She's already jumping up and down, shaking her hands and turning her neck. She's in full game mode. Without opening her eyes she starts speaking to us.

"Do you smell that?" She says, smelling in the air deeply. "That's the smell of fear." She opens her eyes and stares us down. "That team over there fears us!" she says, pointing across the court-yard. "Look at them! They FEAR US!" We all look over. I see fear alright, but not of us. Valentine is marching in front of them, yelling and looking like a crazy lady. Everyone on the team looks like they would like to be anywhere else but there. Fourth is the only one that looks calm. Perhaps I need a therapy animal, maybe a chipmunk.

"They have reason to fear us," Columbus continues. "We are going to dominate this today. DOMINATE!" She screams. She starts running around, pounding us all on the shoulders. Her energy is infectious and I start to get excited. Before long, we're all in a crowd jumping up and down except for April, who is standing off to the side pouting. Santa points to the crowd, telling her to get in, so she walks to the outer edge and puts a hand in. I really hope she's on board with this.

As we continue getting pumped, we hear a sound coming from the speakers set up at the top of the stairs. Fairy and Frost are standing there waiting for the competition to commence. Trumpets blare a royal song. We all stop and stare. "This is going to be interesting," Shadow whispers to me. I have no clue what she's talking about, but then I hear a proclamation go out through the sound system.

"Ladies and Gentleman, please gather at the bottom of the stairs as we await His Royal Highness." Both teams start to make their way over. I'm sure our screams are still echoing in the ears of our opponents. Valentine shoots April a look of absolute betrayal. Poor girl, it must be hard being separated from her minion. Valentine will have to survive on her own, oh, the horror. A silence falls over us as the trumpets sound again.

"Hear ye, hear ye," a voice booms. "All hail KING BUNYAN!" With that, another song trumpets out, causing Fairy and Frost to look towards the front doors of the school. Coach is wearing a red and green robe, with a matching crown, making his way to the front. In his right hand, he carries a jeweled scepter. Capping off this regal outfit is the fact that he is still wearing his too-tight shirt and his too-tight sweats. I've never seen anything like this in my life.

Our "King" stops at the front of the steps and turns slowly around with his arms up in the air. After a full 360, he stops to soak in the adoration of...well... I don't really know who. He signals us for silence, even though we aren't making any noise at all. In fact, we're frozen in total stunned silence, but it doesn't seem to faze him.

"My royal subjects," he announces in his booming voice, only this time it has a hint of an awful British accent. "We are gathered here today-eith for the most glorious-eith of all competitions. Our teams will face-eith off in a race of extreme-eith proportions. I, King Bunyan, will be the judge-eith, ruler-eith and watcher-eth of the race. ALL HAIL YOUR KING!" His arms rise again and we all look at each other, not knowing what to do. Coach doesn't seem to notice and his eyes are closed with the biggest smile on his face, truly soaking it all in.

"Now take a knee, subjects," he says, lowering his arms. Confused, we all gingerly lower ourselves down. Shadow has been pitching a fit the entire time and this sends her over the edge into hysterics. "Look at me. I'm a royal subject kneeling before the king," she says, oozing with sarcasm.

Coach's smile goes away, and he looks us over. "My subjects, this is a serious matter. If anyone is caught cheating during the Holiday Battle, they will be sentenced to death! They will be BEHEADED BY SWORD!" He then takes his thumb and runs it across his throat. Fairy clears her throat from behind him and he lowers his hand quickly. "I mean, you will be in big, big trouble," he says. "Now rise, my subjects."

We all rise gingerly. "Remember, subjects," Coach goes on. "All members of your team must be present before you start the puzzle. Teachers will be at every stop to make sure you aren't cheating. If you are cheating, you face the guillotine and it will be OFF WITH YOUR HEAD!" He quickly looks back at Fairy's frowning face. "Ha ha, just kidding. Now, subjects, gather yourselves and get ready to embark-eith."

I see Columbus, Santa, and others start to stretch and limber up. I try to do the same, but I come across more like a sapling flailing in the wind. I take a look at the faces around me. They all look serious. Even April's smugness is replaced by stoniness. I take a deep breath and start jumping like I've seen Columbus do a million times. I feel my limbs loosen, blood flowing. It's now or never.

"My royal subjects, it's time," Coach announces, still committed to the terrible accent. For a brief second I take this all in. I clear my eyes and make my heart full. I bow my head and wait. "COMMENCE!" Coach screams and we're off.

We head in one direction following the red markers while the other heads in the opposite direction following the green markers. The trail takes us around the side of the school, past where the bonfire was and down a hill. The hill is huge and I've been told stories since my arrival about death sledding. But now we're at top speed, barreling down, headed for the table set up at the bottom. Reaper is standing beside it, his black robe blowing in the wind. We all arrive at the same time and we surround the puzzle.

"Flag, what do you see?" Santa asks. When we had our planning session after the selection, it was determined that Flag would take the lead with the puzzles and we would try to help if we could. Knowing the level of intellect running through Flag's head, I doubt if anyone will need to help him.

"We need to shuffle the pieces together to form a picture," Flag says in deep concentration. "The key is to start in the top left corner and work your way around. Once the first part is in place, the rest should move quickly.

"GOTCHA," Santa says. "What do you need us to do?" Flag stops, cracks his knuckles and stretches. "Just stand back and get out of my way."

With that, we back up and he attacks. He works at an astonishing pace, rearranging pieces in all directions. Everyone's standing back to give him space except April, who's watching the puzzle. At one point, Flag stands up and rests a hand on his chin. Panic sets in, as I think he must be stuck. Just then I see April lean over and say something to Flag. He looks at her and a smile breaks out on his face.

He gives her a bear hug, which is hilarious because it's obvious April was not expecting it. He releases the red-headed dead fish in his arms and goes back to the puzzle. His hands move, swipe, swipe, slide, shift, and move even faster than before. He stands up, looks at Reaper and declares, "DONE!" We all rush to the table to see the HH logo displayed. Reaper looks over the puzzles.

"You are finished," he says. Before he can change his mind, we're running back up the hill. Which is hard, let me tell you. Fall, Columbus, and Santa make it to the top with ease, but others like myself and Shadow are struggling. When those at the top see this, they head back down to help. Santa loads me on his back, Shadow on Fall's, and they carry us up the mountain.

When we get to the top, I ask for onions, but no one gets my joke. I'm expecting a few minutes to catch my breath, but no, we're off and running right away. It looks like we're making a giant circle around the grounds of the school. We run forever, or about six minutes, until we make it to a tall wooden wall with ropes hanging down it.

St. Nick is waiting there for us. "Congratulations, red team. You have beaten the green team here." We let out a cheer and wait for his instructions. "This test is to see how well you work as a team. It's three different stages. The first part of your team will begin by climbing the top of the wall, where they will grab a bag with the puzzles. They will strap the bag to their back and climb back down. The second group will grab the pieces and race them to the last group on your team.

This third group will take out the pieces and assemble the puzzle. When the puzzle is complete and I declare it correct you may move on. Since there is an odd number, you must decide which stage will have one less student. Do you understand?"

We all nod and break into our groups. I end up on the Puzzle team with Flag, April, and Shadow. Shadow is very happy because she knows Flag will handle it. Our runners are Columbus, Spring, Pres, and Patrick. Columbus wanted to climb with Santa and Fall, but J.J. kept saying, "I'm so fast like a monkey. Let me climb." So she took the final spot. They decided whoever made it back down first would go right back up. I made my way over to the puzzle area, leaving the climbers and runners to start. St. Nick raises his hand, looks us all over, and shouts, "GO!"

The first part is the J.J. show. Boy, can she fly! When she said she was a monkey, we all laughed. Not now. Not while watching her scale the rope in a third of the time the boys do. She's already back on the ground handing the bag to Columbus as Santa and Fall reach the top. She turns off one foot, twists in the air and lands back on the wall in one motion, never letting go of the rope. She's back up in a flash, then back down just a fraction behind the others. Monkey is an understatement.

Columbus arrives first, shoving the bag hard into Flag's chest. "Move it!" She yells. Flag runs to the table and dumps his pieces. The other runners arrive all at once. I'm presented a bag from Pres and I take off to join the puzzle.

Right about that time, the green team arrives and St. Nick starts explaining to them about the competition. I notice that Turkey has a bandage on his head and I start to wonder what happens at the next stage. I've no time to focus on that as I'm too busy standing over the puzzle and acting like I'm helping. It wouldn't matter, as April and Flag are well on their way. This time, the puzzle seems to spell something out. The rest of our team waits anxiously. The green team is starting to climb the wall, which makes Columbus panic. "Flag! Come on!" She screams. Flag turns around and holds one finger to his mouth, "SHHH!" We all laugh, but Columbus just fumes. She's just a tad competitive.

I hear the other team running towards us and now the lead is diminishing. They arrive and start putting their puzzle together. "Don't blow this, April," I hear Valentine call out. If it rattles April, you can't tell; she's focused. The other team is dumping their pieces on their table when April and Flag's arms go up. "DONE!" April shouts. St. Nick has made his way down by us. He goes to the table and looks it over. We all rush to see the puzzle reading. "ALL HAIL THE MIGHTY KING BUNYAN." Really? "It's correct," St. Nick says, and we're off.

I look back and see the green team is close to finishing the puzzle. "We need to hurry," I say. We all kick it up a notch and move it to the other side of the school. As before, Shadow and I are left behind, but thankfully, we don't arrive too late behind. We find ourselves standing in front of a pile of presents.

"Ho! Ho! Ho!." Shadow announces. Ms. Grimm is standing by the pile smiling like she usually is. "Oh, welcome, welcome, welcome, "She says. "You guys look so cute in your uniforms.

Give me a hug." Before we can say no, Grimm is pulling us all toward her for a big embrace. I see Columbus's face turn red, she really wants to win this. After Grimm lets us go, she finally addresses us.

"These presents here make a pyramid. You must build the pyramid correctly and carry it across to the tree over there." She says pointing to a Christmas tree about fifty yards away. "If you drop your pyramid or any present tumbles off you have to come all the way back here to the beginning and start over. When you reach the tree and place them underneath you may continue on. Be careful of the presents falling. We have had some injuries." I stifle a laugh, picturing Turkey getting bonked on the head.

I run over to the presents with the others and we start sorting them out. "They are all different sizes, " Flag states. "We need to get the most solid ones on the bottom and the lightest one on top."

"Whatever we do we need to do it fast," Columbus says, starting to pile presents on top of each other. She's ignoring Flag and you can see she's not doing it right. "Hold on, Columbus." We all stop and look at April. She's actually talking to us. "Remember, we have to carry this as a team to the tree. It needs to be solid and stable. And this," she says, marching over to where Columbus is working, "It isn't solid and stable, like at all."

"Show us how to do it, April; take the lead," Patrick says. He and I exchange a glance that seems to say, "Wow." April starts to direct Fall and Spring to the biggest ones to form the bottom. J.J., Shadow, and I started piling up the smaller ones to one side. Flag and Santa are starting to place the medium-sized ones on the base that the twins are making, but April stops them. "That's going to be hard to lift. Let's try holding up the base, then putting the presents on it. " Everyone works at this except Columbus and me.

We are the tallest ones, and we're designated to place the presents in their places. Our group holds up the base and we gently put the medium presents on it. Then Columbus lifts me on her shoulders and I place the smaller presents on top. Before we know it the pyramid is built and we're ready to go.

Columbus joins the group holding up the packages and I'm told to guide us. Why me? I don't want this pressure. They start out and I do the best I can to remind them to go slow and steady. Columbus is screaming to go fast, so most my job is keeping her under control. About halfway through, our top starts to wobble. I yell, "Stop!" Just in time, too, as the top package is inching its way towards falling off. Columbus lets go of her part and I climb back onto her shoulders. " Do it quick, Arbor!" she says, moving us to towards the pyramid. "Slow down, Columbus," I cry. She's going too fast and when I reach for the top package, I start to slip off her shoulders. Before I know it, I'm headed down, and I try desperately to stop myself. I reach back and grab a handful of Columbus's hair to try to stay on. "OUCH!" She screams, letting go of my legs. That's the final momentum I needed and I crash on top of the pyramid, causing the presents to fly everywhere.

I fall down hard on my right shoulder and pain shoots through me. I roll over screaming, the other presents start tumbling on me. I use my other hand to shield my head so I don't end up with matching bandages to Turkey.

After the collapse settles, my team digs me up and Ms. Grimm is there in an instant to check on me. "Oh, dear!" she cries. "Is your shoulder okay?" I try to lift my right arm and pain roars through my shoulder. I look at Ms. Grimm, shaking my head. Columbus appears next to me and swoops my good arm over her shoulders. "I'm so sorry, Arbor," she says. I see that tears are starting to well up in her eyes. "I'm so, so, so sorry. I got in such a hurry that I... I....." She stops speaking, getting really quiet.

"We need to get you to Mother Goose right now," Grimm orders. I take a look at the rest of my team standing there, looking more concerned with me than the competition, and it makes my heart swell. Here we're trying to do something that has never been done before and their main focus is me, not winning.

"If it's okay, Ms. Grimm. I'd rather wait until we finish and then go see the nurse," I say softly. She looks at me with a huge smile and nods. I turn to the rest of the team. "Now get going," I order, wincing with pain.

"Are you sure you don't want to go see Goose?" Patrick asks. I shake my head. "I want to finish with you guys." Now a Grimm-sized smile comes across his face. "You heard her," Patrick says. "Let's move it."

I make my way to the side and stand with Grimm as my team starts the process of moving the packages back to the beginning. I watch helplessly as they stack them again, this time with Shadow on top of Columbus. "If you drop me, Columbus, I swear I will do more than grab your hair," she says.

My team makes quick work this time as they make the trek to the tree. They place the presents underneath and we start to make our way back to the finish line. None of us are running as we know it's useless. The green team will have finished a long time ago. I'm being helped along gingerly by Spring and Columbus, who keeps apologizing to me over and over. We pass around the bend when Fall takes off in a full sprint. Screaming something at the top of his lungs. We all stop and try to figure out what is going on when Santa yells, "No one is there!" Sure enough, standing at the top of the stairs is only Fairy, Frost, and King Bunyan. Everyone starts to take off, leaving me and my two helpers behind. Columbus gives me a look and I say, "Go for it." She smiles and takes off in a flash. "I'm not leaving you," Spring informs me.

"Why am I not surprised?" I reply. "But we need to move it. By some dumb luck, the green team isn't there and I don't want to lose because of me." Before she starts mothering me, I take off at a slow trot. My shoulder is killing me, but I fight through the pain, imagining the look on Valentine's face when she sees that we have won. Spring runs beside me the whole way. I'm sure she's afraid I'm going to pass out. But I don't.

Spring and I make it to the top of the stairs, joining our teammates in victory. Holy tree stump, we won! Everyone is jumping around, celebrating the win. Fairy rushes to me right away when she sees me tilted to one side. "Let's get you to Goose right now," she says. Spring goes with me inside. I glance back one last time at my team. We won the first round. Change is coming.

CHAPTER FIFTEEN

Goose bandages me up and I'm able to join my team in time for dinner, which is awesome because it's pizza muffins, and I'm starving. My team stands and cheers for me as Spring and I enter the dining hall. I blush hard as I go to take my seat. Much to my absolute surprise, April is sitting with us. This warms my heart. She was amazing today.

I'm filled in with the rest of the afternoon. Our team stood around for almost an hour waiting for the green team to arrive. Finally, as the sun was going down and the temperature dropped, Frost was sent to retrieve them. After about fifteen minutes we see Valentine coming around bend by herself. Needless to say she looked rather unhappy. Her team finally came walking along, looking dejected. In fact, they are making Frost look downright skippy compared to their faces. Even Fourth looked ragged, hard to believe it but even Pop looked done with today.

When they make it back to the finish line, Bunyan asks them what happened and Valentine snapped. "They couldn't figure out the puzzle!" she yelled, pointing at the group. "How hard can a puzzle be!?"

"Let me guess," Flag said. "You got about halfway through and then you saw no other options?"

"That's right." Sarge said, finally breaking the team's silence.

"What did you do?"

"I didn't do anything," Flag answered. "It was all April."

"WHAT!?" Valentine screamed. "Is that true?" Valentine marched up to April and got right in her face. "Why did you help them?"

April turned the color of her hair and didn't seem to know what to say. She tries to mouth something, but only noises are coming out.

"You need to back off right now." It's Fall who speaks and steps in front of April.

Valentine doesn't move; she just stares down Fall.

"I said move," Fall told her again. Valentine stayed there for a few more seconds until Frost approached her and gently moved her away.

I'm stunned listening to this. The nerve of Valentine. No wonder April was now sitting with us. I sneak a glance at the Big Four table and watch as Valentine is in a deep talk with Turkey. Never have I seen her so serious.

That night, I make a call to my parents to relay to them that I'm okay. They had already heard from Goose, but I wanted to keep them calm. Being an only child has its duties. One of those is keeping parents off the ledge. "We are going to get on the next flight and come out there," my mom says into the phone.

Oh my goodness! Really? "There's no need to do that, Mom," I say. "I'm fine, and Goose is taking good care of me." Plus, I don't need two moms here at school. I already have Spring waiting on me hand and foot.

"But you have never been hurt and away from me."

I roll my eyes and laugh. But she's right. Every knee scrape, paper cut, and twisted ankle has been fretted over by her. I know I need to distract her with something, get her mind off the injury.

"Mom, I really am okay," I tell her. "All my friends here are doing their best. I'm well cared for." That does the trick as I hear a small gasp on the other end. "Oh, Arbor," she says, and I recognize the tears in her voice.

"What's wrong?" That's my dad and I hear him take the phone. "Arbor, what's happening? Your mother is crying."

Again, I roll my eyes and sigh. "Dad, nothing is wrong. I was just telling her not to worry. All my friends here are taking care of me," I tell him.

"Friends?" he says, "Did you hear that? Arbor has friends!"

"Oh my gosh, you make it sound like I'm a total freak," I laugh into the phone.

"It's not that, honey," He says back to me. "I'm just happy to hear you admit that people like you. Wait.....these are real actual people, right? Not made up in your head, friends?"

"Dad!" I squeal at him. "Yes! They are real, actual people." I go on to tell him about Spring smothering me all day.

A sudden sadness that I didn't know was in me surfaces. I really miss my parents. All the letters, emails, and phone calls in the world couldn't match what it means to be with them in person. Having them encourage me over the phone isn't the same as being there. As much as I've felt I've grown while here, nothing can replace being with your parents, who love you, in person.

I was so focused on myself that I never stopped to think about how it must be affecting them. I know they have been spending more time doing holiday promotions, which is hard for them to do when they have a teenager living with them. But it has to be hard going from having me there to being alone. They don't even have a Frost to torture them.

"Promise you won't fly across the country?" I ask my dad. He laughs and promises. We all say "mushy stuff" and hang up. I feel some tears coming, but I hold them back. If my parents can handle their world being changed, then so can I. Spring makes sure I have everything I need for the night and I have to practically push her out of my room. I lay down and start to think about my day. But I don't get far as sleep takes me.

The next afternoon we're back standing in front of the steps of the school. The green team is looking focused and serious. I guess the embarrassment from yesterday's defeat has inspired them today. My team is loose and relaxed. Even Columbus is smiling. She woke me up this morning with more apologies; she also swears that her competitiveness will be under control. I tell her I don't want her to change who she is but maybe bring it down eighty-two notches. So this is where we find ourselves. If we win today, then the Holiday Cup is ours.

At that moment, music blares through the speakers. A serenade of bagpipes plays, bringing our attention to the top of the stairs. Coach Bunyan makes his appearance...oh boy. This time Coach is decked out in a red and green kilt, red sash, and his face is painted half green, half red. He is carrying a big sword, and yes, he is still wearing his normal coach wear. "You have got to be kidding me," Shadow says, causing our team to bust out in laughter. When Coach reaches the top of stairs, he lifts the sword and yells, "VICTORY!"

The music continues to play as Coach marches back and forth, screaming about battling your enemies through the trenches of life. He rambles for about ten minutes until Fairy finally steps forward. With a final cry of, "FREEDOM!" He explains to us that today is a scavenger hunt around the grounds of the school. Teachers are placed in different sections. We will open our first clue here and try to figure out where on the map to go. Each clue will lead us to another teacher until we have visited each one.

The first team back will be declared the victor. My team and I gather in a circle with the first clue, awaiting the signal. I sneak a glance towards Valentine and we lock eyes. She throws a smirk my way and I look away. We are going to win this!

We don't win.

We make our way back to the start after completing the hunt

in what we think is a fast time, but as we turn back towards the front steps the green team is already there. They let out a huge cheer when they see us coming in second. Valentine herself seems especially proud. All the rage she felt yesterday is replaced with arrogance and mockery. What really surprises me is how much the other Minors are enjoying the victory. Only Mem seems to be reluctant to rub it in our faces. Even Pop is running circles around us, barking.

As a team, I'm proud of us. While we're all stunned that we lost, we don't get mad or upset. Columbus holds it together as best as she can in the face of defeat. She stays quiet, but I see the rage in her eyes as Valentine and the others dance around. We gather ourselves and head in to clean up. We leave the green team to their celebration.

That night is spent hanging out in my room. J.J. seems to be acclimated to us and is entertaining Spring, Columbus, Shadow, and me with stories of Taiwan. "The food in America is so good!" she's telling us. "In Taiwan, we have stinky tofu that smells like a toilet." We all look at each other and crack up. "I mean, it smells like the stuff in the toilet." J.J. holds her nose and makes a funny face, sending us all rolling to the floor. My goodness, I've become another cliché. I'm rolling on the floor laughing. J.J. starts demonstrating to us a dragon dance when we hear a soft knock on the door. Spring opens it to find April outside.

Spring lets her in, and we can tell instantly that she has been crying. Spring, being the mother that she is, hugs her right away and brings her to sit with us. "What is wrong, April?" April is having trouble speaking. Like before, she's trying to say something, but only strange noises keep coming out. All we can make out in the garble is the word "Valentine," but for us, that's all we really need to hear.

After a bit, April calms down and explains to us that she went to Valentine's room to hang with her like normal, but when she got there, Mardi and the other girls from the green team were there. Valentine told Mardi to inform her that she was not welcome in the room. With that, she breaks down again. All of us except J.J. have experienced the wrath of Valentine. So April has come to the right place. Part of me feels the blame for this since she never asked to be selected by our team.

We spend the rest of the night doing our best to cheer up April. By the time we all break apart for bed, she seems to have recovered some. Spring walks April to her room, telling her the whole way that everything is going to be alright.

For the first time in two days, we have our regular school schedule since the final stage of the competition takes place at night. That's the talk of the school today as it seems that no other competition has every ever been held outside at night. The fact that Frost is the creator of this one only adds to the intrigue.

All day in Track, Valentine sits off by herself and won't even acknowledge anyone. April looks terrible, like she didn't sleep at all last night. I find myself slowly getting angrier as the day goes on. It's not right for April to be treated this way, even if Valentine feels abandoned. By the time we head to the assembly hall for the competition, I've made it my mission to win this thing, hurt shoulder and all. As I'm about to enter the hall, I see Fairy motion me over to where she's standing with Goose. I leave the others and make my way over. As I approach, I see serious looks on their faces. This can't be good.

"Hello, Arbor," Fairy greets me. "How are you feeling today? How is the shoulder?" Goose stands there wringing her hands and looking at me with worry. "It's great," I lie. "I'm ready for the next competition."

"That's great, dear," Goose says. "Can you lift your shoulder and rotate it around for me?" I take the sling off and I start to raise it. About a quarter of the way up, pain hits me, and I let out a yelp. I see Fairy and Goose exchange a look and I know what is coming. "Arbor," Fairy says. "You're not going to be able to compete tonight. I'm not going risk further injury, even if it for the Holiday Cup."

I must have looked as bad as I felt because both Fairy and Goose embrace me. I fight back the tears as my head is buried in Goose's crazy gray hair. They let me go, and I walk into the hall to join my team. I fill them in on what is happening. They try their best to be encouraging, but I feel like that I'm letting them down. We don't have much time to discuss it because at that moment all the lights go out.

CHAPTER SIXTEEN

We sit in the dark for what seems like an hour or thirty seconds, but in the dark, I can't tell how long. "Creepy," whispers Shadow. The school does have a creepy vibe going on right now. The assembly hall doesn't have any windows, and really the only light is coming from watches and the emergency lights. Shadow laughs and starts to let out a low growl when music starts to play and two spotlights hit the middle of the stage.

"Is life getting you down?" A voice booms over the PA system. "Are you tired of trying to get ahead but always being left behind?" The spotlights start to move around the stage, being added by a light show of all different colors. "I've come to you today to let you know that you're a winner. You can do anything." The lights and music stop leaving us in total darkness again.

Suddenly the spotlights hit the stage and standing there is Coach with his back to us. He turns around and seems to be wearing a suit jacket over his clothes with a headset microphone looped around one ear. There is a red flower sitting behind the other ear. He lifts his hands and speaks, "You are FANTASTIC!"

Again the lights and fast music hit and Coach starts walking back and forth. Pointing to everyone he keeps booming "You are fantastic! You are fantastic! We are all FANTASTIC!" He then starts jumping up and down declaring all of us to be "FAN-TASTIC WINNERS!" The motivational speech continues on with Coach comparing us all to caterpillars who morph into butterflies. Fantastic butterflies. Finally, he calms down and starts to look serious.

"Listen, my butterflies, tonight is going to be intense!" He takes a deep breath. "The surprise competition tonight is..... ENDURANCE!" I don't know what kind of reaction he was expecting, but we're all too silent to speak. Coach then kisses the tips of fingers and floats them up into the air. Slowly he walks around the stage.

"Outside you will find set up a most treacherous competition. Our own Jack Frost has designed this to push you to the limit. To see how far your mind, body, and spirit can go." I see everyone in the room tense up. I'm sure we're all thinking the same thing; with a mind like Frost's, there is no telling what is in store for us. I glance over at Valentine and see the same concern as everyone else. She doesn't seem confident today.

"Because of the injury that Arbor suffered she's not cleared to compete today," Coach continues. "Therefore the green team must choose one member to sit out and decide now before we go out." The green team huddles up and starts to discuss. Valentine and Turkey are going back and forth about who should be that member. They finally break and announce that Mem will be sitting out. The small, frail girl looks absolutely relieved to not have to participate. With that settled, we're dismissed and finally make our way to the back of the school.

Greeting us in the back is blinding light; as in there are giant spotlights set up shining down on the competition. There are twenty blocks of ice set up in a circle. Above those are buckets with handles in front of them. The contraption seems to be built together, a ladder is in front of each block of ice. Again, I silently find myself thankful for my injury. Standing ominously in the middle of the circle is Frost. You can hear nothing but silence as we head toward him. It's like we're frozen in time. Pun intended.

"You will now listen to me," Frost begins. "You will each stand on a block of ice and grab the bar above you. That bar is connected to a bucket of water. Once you have grabbed the bar you will lift it off the connector and then the only thing supporting the bucket is you. You will hold on as long as you can, you will strive to push yourself as far as you can go, and you will win the challenge for your team and the Holiday Cup if you're the last one standing." The silence that follows speaks volumes.

The teachers of the school start positioning themselves in front of the blocks. Stacks of towels, blankets, and dry clothes are set up. I notice off to the side are benches and changing stations with heaters positioned around them. Santa gathers our team close together. I stand between Spring and Shadow. Spring grabs my free hand, and I will my strength into her.

"Hey, chill out, guys," Santa says, smiling. The reaction is priceless. "That's the best you can come up with?" Shadow hollers at him. "Hey, don't be so cold to me," he quips back. "She can't help it," Patrick says. "She's cold-hearted."

That does it and we all start cracking up. Spring suggests a prayer and we all bow our heads together. As she says the words I feel closer to these people than anyone ever outside my parents. What a special moment. We break and I watch my teammates make their way up the ladders and get into their positions. They are about to face the ice, wind, water, and cold all while wearing sneakers, sweats, and a t-shirt. I'm led away to sit on the benches by the heaters, and I'm soon joined by Mem. She's already shivering as she sits down on the green team's bench. Poor girl. I don't know how she would have managed this feat. I look over at her and smile. I like Mem.

All Holiday High students are standing and getting ready. Suddenly, it hits me. I don't want to be sitting here, away from my team nice and toasty in the warm. I need to be down there with them. I may not be up on a block of ice, but I want to help in any way I can. I get up and make my way over to Mem. I explain what I'm doing, and I offer my hand. She hesitates and doesn't look like she wants to move at all.

"Come on, Mem. Labor is over there." I say to her hoping that the realization of her little brother standing on a giant block of ice will move her. "We will get you a blanket and wrap you up."

"I'm only going to cheer for Labor and Fourth," she tells me. "I don't want to be considered teammates of the others." I nod my approval, and we make our way towards the circle. We grab a blanket, and she heads down to stand in front of Labor. I look at my team.

"Whoo! Arbor is here to freeze with us," Columbus shouts. "*ICE* to see you!" Shadow calls, making a groan erupt from the others. "Listen," I say addressing them. "I'm not good with words." That gets a big chuckle from Patrick. I give him a look and continue. "But I just want to say that you guys are awesome. You are all fantastic butterflies." That gets them laughing and I know that me being here is going to help. "Just don't freeze to death and, uh, try to win, I guess."

"Now that's motivation, folks!" Santa laughs.

Frost calls us to silence. He instructs the students to grab the bar above them and release the hold. I make eye contact with Patrick and give him a smile. He shakes out his limbs and grabs his bar. Frost counts down from five and they all pull the bar off.

"AAAAAGGHH!!!!" We hear a scream right away and notice that Mardi's bucket has already dropped and she's standing there with her blonde curls soaking wet. One down already.

Goose makes her way over to her and engulfs her in a blanket. It must not be too cold since I see the ice blocks starting to melt. I make my way over to Flag, thinking about this insight.

"How you holding up, Flag?" I ask. He smiles down at me. "Only been thirty seconds, Arbor. I'm good."

"Hey, I noticed that the blocks of ice are melting. It may be by design or just natural, but I think that's going to make your footing difficult." I see Flag's face twist into that look he gets when he calculating something in his head.

"You're right," he says. "As the ice weakens, it's going to shift. Some parts will fall off in big chunks, the block overall will get smaller, and this could happen anytime. It's definitely going to be tricky. If you're not aware of it, then you could easily slip."

"And that means you will be taking a bath right?"

"Correct," he answers.

"So this is something I should tell our team?"

"Absolutely."

So I'm off. I make my way to each member filling them in on what I discovered and Flag's warning to be ready for the ice to shift and get smaller. Only about five minutes into the challenge, my team is looking strong. So far, Mardi is the only eliminated person. She's currently wrapped up in a blanket sitting by herself on the green team bench.

The competition hits the ten-minute mark before we start to see people feeling the pain. Our team takes two hits as J.J. and Spring both drop their buckets. They climb down the ladders and I'm there to help pass out the dry goods to them. J.J. just keeps saying over and over that "Taiwan isn't cold." Spring looks frustrated with herself, but it's short-lived as we hear a cry and see that Eve's bucket has dropped too.

Fifteen minutes in and four are down. Two on each team. I continue to walk by my team, offering words of encouragement. Shadow is feeling it hard as we head into the twenty-minute mark. Her arms are shaking from holding the bar while her legs are shaking from the cold beneath her. As I'm making my way around, I see that what Flag was saying is true and small chunks of ice are starting to fall off. Sure enough, Bunny tries to lift his feet a little to get some relief and he slips. He rights himself, but it's too late, and his bucket falls.

We're coming up on the thirty-minute mark. I start to see and hear the torture that some of the students are enduring. I survey our team and see that Columbus, Patrick, Santa, and Fall are holding strong. Fall looks like he hasn't moved, and he's on a different planet right now. Maybe he's asleep? His eyes are closed and he's not moving at all. Flag is the next to go for us. He joins the others on the red team bench so he can warm up by the heaters. It looks like Pres and April are feeling the pain. I'm so proud of Shadow, as she's visibly hurting but not giving up.

The other team isn't holding up as well as they lose Kris, Turkey, and Hallow within minutes of each other. Leaving only Fourth, Labor, and Valentine giving them the chance to win. Out of those three, Fourth looks solid. Mem has been doing a great job encouraging them all night. The ice is getting bad now, with large chunks cracking and breaking. I see that Patrick's block is getting lopsided, causing him to lean to one side, kind of like he's climbing down an iceberg sideways. It's at the forty-five-minute mark that our team loses both Pres and Shadow.

My team applauds as both their buckets spill. Our seven-foot coach goes and helps Shadow down, carrying her over to get dry. Pres refuses help even though I can see his legs shaking as he climbs down his ladder. I go over to tell Shadow how proud I am of her and she's making jokes about being a popsicle. That tells me everything I need to know; she's fine. I hug her tight before she and Pres join the others. When the first hour passes by, we have five left to the green team's three.

Our advantage doesn't last long. In the span of a half hour, we lose April, Patrick, and Columbus. Columbus comes off her ladder in a rage. "I barely moved my arms at all," she says refusing to even take a towel. Patrick helps April over to the benches, the poor girl gave it her all. I could see in her face as she glances back at Valentine that she really wanted to outlast her former best friend.

We are getting close to two hours. Fall has yet to even show an ounce of pain, but Santa is fading fast. I'm joined in front of them by Patrick and we take turns telling Santa that it's okay to stop, that no one is going to be upset. It's two on two now as Labor finally gives in. Both teams applauded him as he makes his way over to the benches. Mem looks so proud and small as she helps her "little" brother over to the heaters. Columbus is still in her wet clothes, walking back and forth in front of the benches.

Valentine and Santa stop at almost the same time. Santa is soaked as he drops to his knees on the ice. Valentine somehow escapes getting wet at all. She, too, refuses any help and stands in front of Fourth, her only team member left. Valentine grabs a blanket and makes a beeline across the circle to Fourth's station. "You better not lose this!" she screams at him.

Patrick and I are joined by Spring in our spot in front of Fall. "Don't listen to her," Spring tells him. "You hang in there as long as you can, no pressure if you can't." Patrick and I agree with Spring and tell Fall that nothing is wrong with stopping. "Don't tell me that," Fall says, speaking his first words of the entire competition. "Tell me to push it. Tell me to not drop. Tell me I have to win it." For the first time, I see his legs shake.

Spring looks at us, "I can't be that mean," she says. But I know someone who can. I turn and wave Columbus over. She trots over, still in her wet clothes, and stands with the rest of us. "Fall has asked to be yelled at and told not to give up," I say to her, putting my hand on her shoulder. Her eyes widen and a smile breaks out on her face. "Columbus. Always, the coach."

With that, Columbus goes into full coach mode. Yelling at Fall, telling him not to stop, that the entire holiday universe is on his shoulders.

"Stop being a girl and man up!" She screams. A small smile breaks out on Fall's face. I see him straighten up and refocus. His eyes still closed, ice still melting, but his legs aren't shaking anymore even though we're approaching two and a half hours.

On the other side, Valentine is still berating Fourth. To his credit, Fourth is taking all her yelling in stride. Pop is at the base of the ladder, barking up at him. Maybe Fourth speaks dog and whatever Pop is saying is more important than what Valentine is barking.

"Fourth, if you lose this, so help me, I will do everything I can to make you a Minor again, "she screams. We suddenly see a flash behind us, and Mem is making her way across the circle. Labor is limping behind her, still wrapped in blankets. "Slow down, Mem," he yells at her. Even though he's over six feet tall, it doesn't look like he's going to stop her.

"What did you say to him?" Mem says, marching right up to her. Labor limps up behind, trying to move her back. She shakes free and steps up in Valentine's face again. "Take that back," she orders.

Valentine takes her attention away from Fourth and stares down Mem. She's a good six inches above her.

"Go away, little girl," she spews back at Mem. "Why don't you take yourself and your little Minor brother and make your way back to the benches? "

Mem starts to swing at Valentine, but Labor grabs her arm at the last moment and pulls her away. "You think you're so much better than all of us," she's screaming. "But you're not. You're just a pathetic excuse for a person. For a holiday that's all about love, you do nothing but spread hate." Well, that wasn't the best thing to say.

Valentine makes a line for Mem, but Labor has positioned himself in front of her. "You need to back off now, V," Labor tells her.

Valentine stops, but she presses right up to Labor. Before we know it, she slaps him hard across the face. Santa runs over, pulling Valentine away. Labor has a red palm print across his face, and now it's Mem who's pulling him away.

Valentine breaks away from Santa and marches right up to Fourth's block. "Listen, you red-headed freak," she yells. "I'm not going to have some stupid group of Minors win this cup and take away my Spring Formal. You will win this or else. Don't cross me or I will make your life miserable."

Pop doesn't take kindly to these words and starts yipping at Valentine's ankles. "Get away from me, you little rodent!" She takes a kick at Pop, hitting him hard on the side. A yelp escapes the animal. Well, that wasn't the best thing to do.

No one knows how he does it, but Fourth throws the bar back over his head and jumps down from the block ice. How does he have the strength to do that? When he lands, he stands up straight, stretching out his whole entire frame. He picks up the ladder and breaks it across the block ice, leaving him holding a big piece of the ladder in his left hand. He starts stalking toward Valentine.

The blood drains from Valentine's face, and her eyes bulge out of her head. She starts to back away but stumbles and falls on her bottom. She turns and scoots away on her knees but it's too late Fourth is standing above her. Just then, a large arm wraps around Fourth's waist, and Coach lifts him away. He wrestles the stick from his hand and takes him over to the side. Valentine collapses on her back, her chest heaving up and down fast.

"Whoo!" A scream escapes behind us, and we turn to see Fall letting his bar go, the water washes over him. Once it slips away, you see a jubilant Fall shaking his hair. "We did it!" he screams. He makes his way down the ladder and Patrick supports him off the final two rungs.

Our whole team is there cheering and clapping. Spring rushes up to give Fall a hug, but he pushes past her through the crowd. He heads straight to April and picks her up. When he lets her down, he plants a kiss right on her lips.

"What the snot!?" I scream and everyone erupts again. Spring looks as shocked as everyone else. Fall finally releases his lips from April's and turns to the rest of us. Fairy has made her way over to us carrying the Holiday Cup, which she hands to Fall. He raises it up and our ovation is heard late into the night.

CHAPTER SEVENTEEN

I survived my first semester at Holiday High. I spend a glorious two weeks at home with my parents. They do nothing but grill me about everything that happens at school. When Spring calls the house to talk one day they spend more time talking to her than I do. I was sad to leave them again but excited to get back and see everyone.

Mentoring with Fairy is the highlight of my day. Despite the fact that we won the Holiday Cup and the teams were different than ever before, the divide among the students has grown even wider. The dining hall is basically just two tables now as Fourth, Labor and Mem have joined us leaving the other eight members of their team sitting at what was known as the Big Four table.

Fairy, Santa, and I spend time daily discussing the history of the council and the future. She pushes us to continue to reach out to all students despite the divide that's growing. Santa came back from break with news that his father was not happy about his role in the Holiday Cup victory.

Spring season has finally made its way to the Holiday High school grounds. The Spring Formal is only a week away and Pairing Week is upon us. Having never been to a school dance before, I never gave two thoughts about who I would be going with to the formal. Pairing Week is a school tradition where the boys of the school come up with crazy, over the top ways to ask girls to the Spring Formal. My friends reassure me that I'm going to be asked, but I still don't count on it.

Pairing Week starts out with a bang. At breakfast Monday morning Fall stands atop one of the empty tables and pronounces that he desires to take the "Magnificent, beautiful, wonderful April to the Spring Formal." He then hits a button and confetti guns go off all over the hall. The bang is loud enough to make Shadow scream out. We are all covered and are picking out confetti from private places for the rest of the day. This pairing isn't a surprise since Fall and April have been so lovey-dovey since the Holiday Cup. If Fall is awake, he's with April.

Valentine is the next to receive the honor of being asked to the Formal. Kris spreads hearts all over the steps leading from the girl's side of the school. When she reached the bottom of the stairs, he had spelled out "FORMAL?" in roses. If Santa finds it awkward that his cousin is asking his ex-girlfriend to the Spring Formal he doesn't make it known. The very next day Santa made his intentions clearly known.

At the end of the morning assembly, Coach Bunyan makes his way out onto the stage dressed in king attire. He holds a scroll in his hand and proceeds to read a poem declaring Santa-eith's desire to ask....SPRING! to her Formal. Spring looks completely shocked and can only nod her answer. The rest of the day finds the rest of our girls teasing Spring about how it is "her" formal.

The other pairings take up the rest of the week. Fourth and Mem, Bunny and Mardi. Flag does a cute scavenger hunt to ask out J.J. Pres and Columbus decide to go as friends. Shadow and Labor will attend together. Each night the girl's tease me that Patrick is gearing up for something huge for me. But at this point, I'm certain that Turkey is going to ask me. But then Turkey asks Eve with a terrible interpretive dance and there goes that.

It's the Wednesday night before the dance and I'm making my way down to the Study Lounge. I'm stressing about the presentation coming up in Time's history class and am looking forward to picking Patrick's brain. I have been assigned the country of Chad. Hopefully, Patrick knows something. All Fall had told me was that everyone in the country was named Chad. He was funnier when he slept all day.

I enter the lounge and stop. Set up around the room are candles everywhere. On the tables, the chairs, the floor, and all along the bookshelves. Standing in the middle of the room is Patrick. Soft music playing over the speakers. I don't know how to act in this situation; these are uncharted waters for Arbor Day.

Patrick has a smile on his face and motions me to come forward. I somehow remember how to walk and head towards him. He just keeps smiling at me. I know that maybe I should return the smile, but I'm afraid that it will just look like a twisted smirk. So I just stand there trying to think of what to say to this. "Do you know anything about the country of Chad?" I ask.

He looks at me weirdly and then laughs. "You, Arbor Day, have such a way with words." Shaking his head he takes both of my hands in his. That sinking feeling in my stomach returns and I feel the closeness between us. Somehow standing this close to someone hurts me, but not in a bad way.

"I know that we're supposed to do some giant show of public adoration when asking you to the formal but I thought this is more our style, being that this is the first place that we met."

My world slows down. I look around and notice the details of the room. Each flame flickering in slow motion, the trail of smoke from one that has burned out, the glow of the dim lights dancing across the ceiling and the shine off Patrick's shamrock necklace. His eyes are twinkling like two embers as the light reflects off them. I notice the heaviness of my breathing. He is speaking, but it's distorted and I can't make out what he's saying. I will my mind to refocus and the world comes vacuuming back to me in a WHOOSH.

"I think you're wonderful, Arbor. A breath of fresh air in an otherwise stale world," he says to me. "So would you do the honor of going with me to the Spring Formal?"

I let my sense come back to me and gain control of my mind. I may be in uncharted waters, but now I'm at least not by myself. Standing here with me is Patrick. The Patrick I met on the first night, the too-bright, conflicted, wonderful, adorably cute red head in glasses. You would think that with all the smarts in his brain, he would know better than to choose me.

"I absolutely will," I say to him and I feel a huge smile come across my face this time.

The next morning Patrick lets it slip casually into conversation that he asked me to the formal. Everyone is so excited and wants to hear every detail. Mem squeals with delight when she hears about all the candles. Fall pops his head up to find out what the commotion was about. We tell him and he replies, "Bout time," and goes back to sleep. So now we all have dates, including me. The dance is on Saturday, I have three days to get ready.

Saturday becomes a tornado of preparation. Tornado may not be the word to describe it. I have never been much of a girly girl, not worrying about makeup and hair. When Spring hears this she can't be stopped from making me her pet project. It's a whirlwind throughout the girl's side of the school. While the boys are out playing baseball, much to the despair of Columbus, I'm sentenced to a whole day of primping and prepping. Packages arrive around noon and we're all surprised with brand new dresses from April's family.

"I promise this isn't a trick," she says, bringing each one to us. Columbus opens her to find a dark shade of green with flowers and bows on it. "I'm not wearing this," she declares. But I can see in her face that she loves it.

Finally, we're all dressed and ready to make our appearance.

My dress is red, with way more of a low cut than I would ever choose for myself. It's long with a slight slit coming up the left side. I look in my mirror and I don't even recognize who I am. Spring is so wonderful. I sigh and think about how much I owe her. I join the other girls at the top of our stairs, ready to make our way down.

The school has a tradition of a promenade on the night of the Spring Formal. Each couple is announced and they make their way down the steps where they meet at the bottom in front of the fireplace. There they pose for a picture.

The theme we chose was "Amongst the Stars," so the school is dimmed and glowing stars are placed all over the walls and ceilings. We also made a path of stars down the steps guiding you to your date. Down at the bottom will be the faculty, and teachers will be decked out in their very best. I hear Coach will forgo his normal attire and is wearing a red suit. The same one he wears every year. The one with COACH stitched on the back. He starts to announce the pairings, and I get chills waiting for my turn.

"Spring Forward and Santa Claus," he announces and I see Santa making his way across the landing of the two halls. He is in a red suit, white shirt, green tie, and his long white hair is slicked back. He nods at Spring and they make their way down. I watch as my friend takes off, glowing and radiant. She has done her short black hair up into a tight bun and is wearing a green dress with red trim. She's stunning. As they reach the last set of stairs, the next couple is announced. "Fall Back and April Fool." Well, Fall didn't oversleep. Coach makes his way through all the couples and Valentine and I are left.

Valentine turns around and eyes me up and down. "Well, if you don't clean up nice," she says in that snotty tone I've learned to know so well. "You know you can shine yourself up and make yourself look all pretty. You may have been able to convince a Major to take you to the formal, but you're still just the new girl here. A Minor."

I look at Valentine and instead of the rage that I used to feel, I feel nothing but pity. She has lost so much this year and now she's trying so hard to hold on to the status she feels entitled to.

"Is it lonely where you live?" I ask her. "Up in that tall tower of yours looking down on all of us?"

I see her fists start to close and her nostrils flare. I think she's about to say something, but then we hear Coach announce, "Valentine Love and Kris Eve." She turns, making sure her curls hit me in the face, and she takes off. I see her scowl turn into a fake smile as she heads out to be adored. I silently wish she trips on the way down.

Then I'm alone. I see Patrick across the way, wearing an all green suit and he gives me a short wave. I wave back and smile, still blown away that I'm standing here about to be escorted to the Spring Formal by the cutest and smartest guy I know. We are announced and I step out.

My breath is lost as I look upon the stars. There are a million out there. Every shape and size you can imagine. Combined, they make such a glow that the lights aren't even needed. The green tint of the light seems to make the air magical. I take my first step, being careful to follow the path towards the bottom.

When I reach the foyer, I turn and make my way over to Patrick. His red hair has been trimmed and he is wearing special green-rimmed glasses for tonight. He seems to be staring so intently that I actually feel like he's looking at a stranger. I turn around trying to see what would cause such a stare and I'm all alone. I turn back and Patrick is pointing at me, mouthing the word, "You." I smile and we make our way to stand in front of the fireplace.

"You look stunning, Arbor," he whispers to me. I love how he always makes sure to say my name when talking to me. He reaches into his pocket and pulls out a green box.

"Are you proposing?" I ask him, only being half serious. He shakes his head and opens the box. He pulls out a shamrock necklace similar to his and he places it around my neck. I feel goose-bumps rise all over my skin as his fingers touch my neck. He's ever so gentle as the necklace is connected. "Thank you," I whisper back.

"Over here, you love birds," I hear Grimm say, and we pose for our picture. We are engulfed in a Grimm grasp and released to join the others in the dining hall, Patrick holding my hand all the way.

Chapter Eighteen

As we enter the dining hall I see that the room is decorated with stars hanging from the ceiling, but whatever is holding them is so thin it looks like they are floating. The room has small tables throughout holding no more than four people each. Muffin has prepared a wonderful meal of muffin-shaped steak and baked potatoes. We are led to our table by Goose, who is dressed up in her prettiest flowered dress.

I see Mem and Fourth seated with Labor and Shadow, even Pop has a little chair pulled up to the table. So I guess technically five can be seated. Our table is right in front of the platform that's set up where the DJ is spinning some soft music. I'm overjoyed to see that we will be sharing our table with Spring and Santa.

The food is divine. No matter how long I've been here I'm still amazed at what Muffin can put forth. Spring is entertaining us with stories of when Fall was little and always napping anywhere they went. "One time we were running all over our church trying to find him and finally discovered that he was under the pew fast asleep."

Patrick tells us stories of this past summer going through the villages of Ireland, helping and serving the communities there.

"That's what I want my holiday to represent here in America." I feel so proud of him at that moment. He looks so mature, like he could take over the holiday right then.

I scan the room and everyone, even Valentine, is enjoying the evening. After the meal the tables are removed and the dancing begins. I stand in a circle trying my best to not look awkward while dancing with the other girls. Coach Bunyan takes over most of the floor showing everyone "how it's done."

Even slow dancing is not as nerve-wracking as I thought it might be. I'm becoming more comfortable with Patrick. The way he holds my hand, holds his hands around my waist, and rests me close to him. I let Patrick guide us around the floor. I'm lost in the stillness of the moment, finding myself not wanting it to end. He puts his face close to mine, our noses touching.

My breath shortens as I know what is about to happen, what I want to happen. The song ends and he takes my face in his hands. Suddenly there is a large light shined on us and Coach yells "Shame, shame, shame."

Mortified, Patrick pulls away from me with a shy smile. "Later," he whispers.

Coach has now made his way onto the platform and is calling us to order. "It's now time to announce the nominees for Spring King and Queen." The crowd cheers and we gather together near the front. Coach is joined on stage by Grimm who is holding the royal garb for the winners.

"Now for our Nominees for Spring King," Coach says. We all hush. "Santa Claus," Coach announces, and I see Santa slowly making his way onto the platform. Now that I know him so well I know he hates this kind of spotlight. Fairy and I have been encouraging him to embrace this part of his life, and to use it to bring the holidays together.

Coach speaks into the mic and announces the next nominee. "Patrick Green." My date squeezes my hand and makes his way to join Santa. "Our final nominee is, pause for dramatic effect." Yes,

Coach actually says the words "Pause for dramatic effect." He does however pause, "Flag Day!" he announces.

I start to clap loudly along with the others from our table. Pres has to push Flag upfront because he's so surprised. I'm so happy seeing Santa, Patrick, and Flag standing up there. Any of them would be a great Spring King.

"Now for our lovely ladies who are vying for your Spring Queen." The applause ceases for a bit as Coach pulls out the cards with the names. "Valentine Love," he announces. Valentine's team does a good job of yelling loudly for her. She's walking to the stage acting like she had no clue she would be nominated. I hope everyone else can see through her phoniness. She takes her place and tries to stand close to Santa which is comical as Santa clearly doesn't want to be next to her.

"Next we have Spring Forward." I erupt with everyone else as Spring actually looks surprised when she makes her way to the stage. Santa leaves Valentine standing where she is and helps Spring up the stairs and onto the stage. He makes a gesture to her and the crowd gets more excited. Coach moves his hands motioning us to settle down.

"We have one more Queen candidate," he says. "Now pause for dramatic effect," which draws a chorus of boos making Coach laugh. "Our last candidate is Arbor Day!" It takes a moment for it to sink in that Coach announced me. Shadow and Columbus have to start pushing me towards the stage. I walk by Pres, Fall, and April who are clapping wildly. I see Pop jumping up and down yapping. I climb onto the stage where Patrick is waiting to help me up the stairs. I look out at my classmates, and I am truly stunned. The lights are bright and I can just barely make out Shadow and Columbus jumping up and down. They should totally be up here not me.

I stand there nervously with all the other candidates and find myself having a flashback to when I was standing in front of the school that first day. I had to convince myself to even walk in. Now

I'm here standing amongst five other people nominated for school royalty. Patrick is now holding my hand in front of everyone and for the first time, I don't freak out when it happens. It feels comfortable, like an extension of myself.

"Now everybody, it's the time we've been waiting for; the announcement of our Spring King and Queen. Can I have the envelope, please?" Grimm hands him a giant red envelope sparkling with green glitter. He makes a big deal of acting like he can't lift it. When he is satisfied that everyone has found his joke funny he finally opens the envelope.

"And our Spring King is Santa Claus!" We all applaud and cheer as Santa sheepishly takes the scepter from Grimm and allows her to crown him. The sash is draped over him and he raises the scepter into the air. "For all holidays!" he proclaims.

When the applause dies down Coach readies himself for the announcement of the queen. "This year's Spring Queen is Spring Forward!" Oh my goodness!! I explode into applause, along with most of the student body.

Spring looks like she's in an entirely different universe. Wide-eyed and dazed she makes her way to the front to accept her royal treatment. The tiara is placed atop her head and she turns to look at me. "What happened?" she mouths and I just applaud louder. No one in this school, on this planet, deserves this more than her. She's a true queen. Not everyone agrees.

Valentine stomps forward and turns Spring around, leaving her back to the crowd. I see Valentine yelling something at Spring while Santa is trying to calm Valentine down and move her back. I can't make out what is being said, but I get the fact that Valentine is very angry at not winning queen. Spring is backing away, trying not to antagonize Valentine more.

Suddenly Valentine reaches past Santa and rips the sash right off of Spring. She makes a lunge for the tiara but Santa restrains her by the waist. I look at Spring standing there totally in shock, with tears forming in her eyes. I notice Columbus trying to run up the stairs and onto the stage.

Thankfully, Pres is holding her back. I look at the rage on Valentine's face, the shock on Spring's, the frustration on Santa's, and something in me snaps.

I walk right over to Valentine, who is now yelling at Santa. I yank the back of her hair and make her face me. Before I know it, my right fist is balled up and I'm swinging with all my might. I connect with Valentine's nose with a hard CRACK! She falls back into Santa's arms, and blood instantly starts gushing out of both nostrils. Patrick grabs me as I'm about to go in for round two and drags me down the stairs. We pass Goose, who is on her way up with a bunch of towels. Columbus is whooping and clapping for me as we hit the bottom of the stairs. She grabs my shoulders and screams into my face, "That was awesome!!!" Not everyone agrees.

I feel a hand on my shoulder and I find myself standing face to face with Fairy and she isn't happy. "My office now," she says with a stern voice that rivals the scariness of Frost.

"I will take her," Patrick offers and Fairy nods. The last I see of the hall, everyone is crowded around Valentine. She's probably loving the attention.

Patrick guides me down the hall towards the office. "Where are you going? Why aren't you dancing? Did you bring me some food?" Sandman says to us as we're passing the foyer. Patrick tries to hold my hand, but they are shaking too badly. What did I just do? We get to Fairy's office and head inside. Patrick sits beside me, my whole body shaking. The adrenaline is racing through me like a strong, angry wind blowing through a forest. I can't calm down.

"She's going to kick me out of school," I say to no one and to Patrick at the same time. All I can imagine is the call my parents are going to get from Fairy explaining that I got into a fight and broke a Major's nose. I can vividly see the disappointed look I will get when I step off that plane when I arrive home. I suddenly feel like

I'm going to throw up, and I figure that's a perfect way to end this night.

Patrick starts to rub my back, but I push his hands away. I don't want anyone touching me now. I don't deserve this great guy supporting me. Patrick starts to say something when we're interrupted by Fairy coming into her office, followed by Frost. Great, Frost.

"That will be all Patrick. Thank you," Fairy says, crossing the room and sitting behind her desk. I see Patrick hesitate, causing Frost to pick him up and start to move towards the door. "You will leave now and go back to the formal," he says.

"You will also leave, Frost," Fairy says, causing Frost to look like he could freeze the whole school. He is about to say something but thinks twice and departs with Patrick, but not before sending me a cold glare. I'm happy to see them both go.

The fewer people I have to see me getting kicked out of the school, the better. I knew I should never have let myself feel hope that I could be happy here. That I could have friends, have a boy actually like me, to think that I could be nominated for anything. That isn't my life. That isn't who Arbor is. I cannot bring change.

I feel my hands start to finally stop shaking and my breathing slows. The sick feeling I was having is still there, joined now by a headache. I move the fingers on my right hand and wince at the pain. Punching someone is overrated. They never tell you how much it hurts your hand.

I won't even look at Fairy. I can't. "Go ahead and send me home," I tell her. My head stays down and I wait for the words. At this point, I just want to leave with no goodbyes, no tears. I just want to be gone. Maybe if I can get out of here quick enough, I won't remember them. Perhaps I can forget.

"Arbor," Fairy finally begins, "I'm not sending you home." I look up at her. She's not sending me home?

"I am, however, extremely disappointed in you." The look that she gives me hurts more than any punch to the nose could. I hang my head down again, avoiding her look. If she won't send me home, maybe I will just go home. Anything to not see that look again. Can someone die from shame? "Arbor, what have I been trying to tell you all year?" she speaks to me softly.

"This whole year, I have been trying to teach you and Santa that bringing the holidays together is the only way to make change happen. Do you have any idea what your actions tonight are going to do for that change?"

I did know. That sick feeling in my stomach is getting more overwhelming, I start eyeing the trash can by Fairy's desk. If I'm puking, then I don't have to answer any questions.

"Arbor!" I look up. Fairy is looking at me with anger now rising to her face. Great. Not only have I disappointed her, but I've ticked her off, too. "What do you think your actions tonight will do to help that change?" she asks again.

"Nothing," I say softly.

"That's right, Arbor," she continues. "Now, I will have to explain to a Major's parents why the newest holiday, who was barely deemed worthy, punched their daughter in the nose, at the Spring Formal. Do you understand the position you have put me in?"

"I understand," I say, barely audible.

"Arbor, I don't think you understand at all," her voice rising. "You were personally selected by me for mentoring. By me, the head of the Holiday Council. They are going to think that this is my influence, which ironically, will hurt my influence. Your behavior tonight was beyond unacceptable. That's what you need to understand, Arbor."

"It's fine. I will leave school," I tell her. It's the least I can do. She's right. Any progress that we have made this year, the teams, the cup, the formal, the breaking down of the social walls, I put all that in jeopardy.

"If it was only that easy," she tells me. "Think about it, Arbor. If you leave school, how much longer will it be until the next time before your holiday will be selected again? No, you cannot leave. You have a responsibility now to your holiday and to your family."

I start to feel anger rising up in me again. She's right, my holiday would be in jeopardy, but you know what? I don't want this responsibility. Under the surface, I realize something that has been there all along. I didn't ask for this, none of this. I didn't want to be here. I didn't ask for her to choose me. I never sought Fairy to be her specially selected mentee. I didn't ask for friends, for a boy to confuse my thoughts. No. The anger is pulsing in me, and I finally look at Fairy and meet her eyes.

"Fine," I say with as much venom as I can muster." I will stay. But don't ask me to be part of your crusade anymore. I don't want to be in your special Mentor group, give me someone else. I will even take Frost. I don't care anymore about this precious change, this all important divide between the Majors and Minors. I want nothing more to do with it. I will stay. I will go to class. I will even take part in the idiotic Confirmation. But leave me alone. I don't need this school, these people, and I sure as HELL don't need a council to deem me worthy."

With that, I stand up and leave the room. I hear Fairy calling after me, but I don't turn back. All I could ever rely on was myself, and that's who I will focus on now.

CHAPTER NINETEEN

The next month I excommunicate myself from everyone. Starting that very night of the Formal I go to my room and refuse to open my door. Finally the knocking stops and I slip into a deep sleep. When I awake I'm more determined than ever that I need no one, nor do I want any one. From now on I protect myself and myself only. I was fine before any of this and I will be fine now.

When I leave that morning I place my headphones in and decide they will not come out. I grab my food and sit alone. Spring immediately picks up her tray and sits with me. I concentrate on my food and the music, ignoring her completely. When Patrick and the others try to come talk to me I leave my food and depart the dining hall. I take one look at Valentine as I pass, seeing that she has a white bandage on her face that seems to brace the nose in place. Her death glare to me is returned by a smile. I want her to know I would do it again.

During my classes I leave my headphones in unless absolutely necessary. I sit away from everyone and take my dinner to my room. That night the knocking returns; they will learn. I don't answer the door. This continues for the week and eventually I'm left alone. There are no more late nights in the study hall and finally no more mentoring with Fairy. I'm assigned to Reaper who gives me the job of sorting and organizing all the clothing for the theater department. Finally something I can do by myself.

My talks with my parents are short and vague. They aren't stupid and know something is wrong but when I refuse to open up they leave me alone. I eat by myself, study by myself and that's all I need. As each day passes I realize exactly how much I let this school get into my head. Arbor Day did not need Holiday High to deem herself worthy. There is a reason I never wanted to come here. I find that girl again, the one that was standing at the bottom of the eight steps trying to find a way to climb them. I find her and I slip her on again like a warm coat.

The middle of April sees the seven-game series pitting the Holiday High baseball team against City High. I attend only because I'm forced to. I sit on the top bench alone, headphones in, and refusing to participate. Baseball is boring anyway. The only time I acknowledge anything is when Columbus gets an inside-the-park home run. She runs with blazing speed around the bases after she hits the ball down the left foul line. When she's headed towards home she jumps over the catcher completely to touch the plate and score. I stand for her. Only her. Not for this school, not for the Fighting Spirit, but for Columbus who shows everyone that she's the best athlete on the field. I'm not totally heartless.

Holiday High wins four games to three. I don't care, I don't attend the victory celebration. So here I am, six weeks into my withdrawal and one week away from the Confirmation. The speaking list has been posted and I see that I'm to present last. Which means I have to sit through all other Confirmation speeches before I can give mine and be released from here. I have no plans to come back. I smile to myself as I think of the ruckus I'm going to cause when my speech is heard. The council, this school, all the parents and Fairy herself will hear exactly how I feel about their precious Majors vs. Minors. My parents will be there and I worry about embarrassing them, but that's what they get for making me come here.

This is where my mind is as I eat breakfast by myself. I'm so into the thoughts of telling Frost exactly what "he will" do that I don't even notice that someone is sitting with me. I look up to see Flag across from me smiling. I shoot him an annoyed look and go back to picking at my food. He doesn't leave. He just sits there smiling and waiting for me to acknowledge he's there. Fine. I take out my headphones and shoot him a look that I hope conveys how much I don't want to speak to him.

"What do you want, Flag?" I snap at him. Flag continues to smile at me. He doesn't say anything just stares at me like he knows a secret. I don't have time for this and I start to pack up my things. "Wait," he says. I stop what I'm doing and I slouch back in my chair.

"I've been watching you," he says. I start to move again but he holds a hand up to stop me. "Not in a weird way, but an experiment. I've been observing and I noticed something. "Ok, he has my attention now. I sit up straight and peer at him. What does this little genius know about me?

"Ok then," I say.

"You are not happy," he says with that same smile on his face. That's it? That's all the super genius has, that I'm not happy?

"Is that what you think?" I ask.

"Yes, Ma'am. You see, over the past three days I've noticed that one, you never smile. Two, you don't talk to anyone, and three, your body language reflects that of someone who slouches, mopes, and kind of shuffles along in this half-walk, half-zombie stumble. You put all those observations together and I conclude that you, Arbor Day, are not happy."

I take in what he says and think through it. His hypothesis has merit. I don't smile, I don't want to talk to anyone. Therefore I don't, and I couldn't care less how I'm walking. My whole goal is to put out the aura of, "Don't talk to me." So he's spot on in his observations. But his conclusion accurate? Am I not happy? I make a checklist of all the things I don't want to be doing right now: attending Holiday High, speaking at the Confirmation, being forced to be part of an age-old ritual that determines my worthiness. So yes, I would conclude that I'm not happy.

I also think about the fact that at night I miss studying with Patrick. I miss the morning prepping with the girls, the nights gathering in someone's room, and letting Spring be mother to all our problems. I miss brainstorming with Santa about new ideas for the Holiday Council to implement. I miss listening to the stories at our table during meal times. I oddly even miss sparring with Valentine. So yes, Arbor Day isn't happy. But I wasn't about to let Flag know that.

"Well, you're wrong," I spit back. "I'm very happy." I even throw him a smile to back it up.

"I don't think so Arbor," he says back to me. "Again, my observations state otherwise. So if my conclusion is that you're unhappy then we need to decide what is going to make you happy. We need to find out what is causing the unhappiness and combat that with happiness. Based on my knowledge of you I have a few ideas."

I could feel that rise of anger coming up in me. I decide to hold it back. I like Flag and it really isn't his fault that I'm bitter at life right now. I look into his earnest face and wish him to leave. There is a reason I've kept everyone away, I'm not worthy of having friends this good. They don't know the real me, the one who hates being here, who never wanted to be here in the first place, the one that mocks them for being a part of this school, this system. I will Flag to leave my table.

"What makes Arbor happy according to Flag Day," he says pulling out notes from his book. "Arbor Day loves her holiday, the training of others into the importance of planting trees and the effect that it has on the world. Arbor Day likes seeing things outside of the box, looking at the world in a different way and expressing it in a unique, too honest way. Arbor Day likes her friends. She likes being with a group of students who are like-minded and dedicated to the same cause." He pauses and looks at me. I shoot him another look, but I have to admit there is less venom behind this one. "Finally, Arbor Day likes Patrick. Patrick makes her happy. He pulls out a photo and passes it over to me.

It's a glossy, black and white shot of Patrick and I at the Formal. The moment captured is from when we were on stage right after I was announced as a nominee. Patrick is holding my hand and my head is leaning on his. I see the shamrock necklace glimmering around my neck. I have a huge smile on my face. I don't recognize the girl in the picture. "So what do we do with this information?" Flag continues on. "The answer is simple. Now that we know what makes you happy, we do those things. It doesn't have to be complicated. Starting with Patrick." I can see him choosing his next words carefully. "Why don't we track him down and see what he's up to?" I think about what he's saying. Do I miss Patrick? Do I truly miss the late night sessions, the closeness I feel when I'm near him, the near kiss at the formal and the promise of one later? I do miss it, miss him. And it makes me mad.

Flag sits there with an eager look on his face. He really expects me to stand up, follow him and track Patrick down, who is probably back in the kitchen helping Muffin with the after breakfast dishes. But I'm not going to follow him. I follow no one but myself now.

I begin to gather my things and leave the table when Flag starts to voice a protest. "Listen, Arbor, I was only trying. "

"NO! You listen," I say, interrupting him. Everyone in the hall stops and looks at the commotion I'm causing. My face is burning and I feel my breathing starting to pick up. I notice everyone staring at me, but I don't care.

"Just leave me alone, okay?" I say to Flag. "I don't care what you think. I don't care about anyone here. You are just a kid freak that everyone puts up with here. Just leave me alone." Well, that did it. I see the tears coming, and I instantly regret what I said. I quickly pack up my things and leave the dining hall. I don't look back.

I'm not sure where I'm headed but I end up going to Reaper's room. I figure I can escape there until after morning assembly when I will be forced to attend class. I enter the room hoping to be alone but find someone already in there playing the piano. I don't recognize her.

I stop to listen, and she's amazing. She's playing effortlessly, hands moving across the keys like lightning. Her talent is mesmerizing. I can't tell how long I had stood listening to her, but she comes to the end of the selection. She slowly turns around on the bench and spies me. She has light brown skin, long black hair, and the most captivating brown eyes I've ever seen. I notice she's not dressed in red and green but is wearing a yellow dress that fits her perfectly even though she's on the heavier side. A wonderful smile breaks out on her face as she stands up.

"Oh, I'm sorry!" she states, coming towards me. "I was told I could wait in here and I saw the piano and I couldn't resist and I didn't know I would be bothering anyone and I'm so sorry and I can leave now if you want." She grabs her bag and starts to head out. I snap out of the piano coma.

"No, no, it's okay," I say. "Who are you?"

"That's so rude of me," She answers and makes her way over to me. "I should have introduced myself and I can't believe I didn't and my parents would be so horrified at my rudeness and I need to make a good impression today and I'm sorry I'm rambling and I'm Cinco and It's so nice to meet you." She sticks her hand out, I take it and shake.

"I'm Arbor," I say back.

"Arbor? You're Arbor Day! You are the newest holiday here, right? And this is your first year and your holiday hasn't been here for decades and I'm here with my parents today and we're hoping that I get in the school for next year and I'm so nervous and isn't this place just the greatest ever?" She says all of this without a single breath. She's very excited to be here. "And I tend to babble on and on when I'm nervous and excited and I'm both now."

Before I know it, a smile breaks out on my face, temporarily putting my guilt and anger over Flag aside. I take a deep breath and answer back. "I'm Arbor Day. I'm the newest holiday here, and this is my first year. Yes, this is the first time in decades that our holiday has been here, and you're here with your parents? Trying to get into school? OH! You're Cinco de Mayo! Oh, wow!"

I really don't know what to tell her about the school. Right now, I don't think the school is the "greatest ever."

"Yes! You know my holiday?" she says. "It's relatively young in this country compared to the other holidays, and that's why I don't think I will get in. But we're here and going to give it shot and my mom says, 'Now, Cinco, you just be yourself and don't babble on' and here I'm babbling on like a crazy girl and I don't really think I can make it here and it would be great if you said something now."

I start to laugh and I see Cinco exhale a little. "She's right, your mom, that is," I tell her. "Just be yourself, don't try to be anyone that you aren't. Fairy loves students that are genuine."

"The Tooth Fairy?" she says, wide-eyed. "You know the head of the Holiday Council?"

"I do, I do," I tell her before she can go on another rant. I know Fairy all too well. I feel another stab of guilt thinking about how long it has actually been since I talked to her. "Fairy is great, and like I said, just be yourself. When you meet with her, just speak from the heart. Don't worry about what you think she wants to hear or try to impress her. Just speak honestly. "

"I just want to go here so bad, "she says. "You must know how I feel, you were just like me a year ago. Holiday High can do so much our family and our holiday and for me and what I want to do in life and all the great holidays that go here and Arbor! I really hope I get deemed worthy."

I look at Cinco and I realize that this is what most holidays feel. The ones that can't come here long to be able to attend Holiday

High. Cinco is viewing this as a life-changing opportunity, a chance for her holiday to reach new heights. I laugh inside as I think back to my parents saying all the same things that Cinco is now saying. Why is it that I didn't, and still don't, feel that way? Maybe I'm the one that's broken, not the system.

I see the stress behind Cinco's smile, and I feel bad. Here is this nice, wonderful, and obviously talented girl who is feeling so much pressure to be perfect so she can gain admittance. I didn't even come when my parents came up to speak with the council. I refused. "Why do you think you won't get in?" I ask her. The smile leaves and I see a serious look come across her face.

"My parents have been working so hard to make our holiday a tradition in America," she says. "But no matter how hard they work we realize that we're still not a native holiday. So not only are we trying to show that our holiday is deemed worthy but also that there are enough Americans that celebrate it. It's something my family has been working at since they took on the responsibility of bringing our holiday to the States." She kind of looks off and I feel like she's playing a movie in her mind.

"Then there is the matter of whether or not they like me and I meet their standards and if I can handle the pressure of being here and..."

"And that you don't babble on right?" I laugh, cutting her off.

"Yes, especially that." She laughs with me.

"Here is what I think," I begin. "If the Council can't see how hard your parents have worked, or how much they want this or how amazing you are then you shouldn't want to be here. It sounds like they're doing great as it is now. Continue that and don't think twice about Holiday High." I see the words I say worry her. "But I think you're going to do fine, Cinco. I really do. Everyone is going to love you." With that, I see her perk up. At that time, her parents and Fairy walk in. Fairy looks absolutely shocked that Cinco is sitting with me.

"*Mami, Papi, hola!*" she says happily. "This is Arbor Day." I greet Cinco's parents warmly and tell them how wonderful their daughter is. I see Fairy looking confused by the whole exchange. She moves Cinco and her parents back towards the hallway, but not until I find myself on the receiving end of a hug from Cinco. It's so fast and heartfelt that I find myself returning it. I fear an uneasy feeling rising in my throat and I think I might cry right here and now. She lets go and thanks me for everything. She heads out to the hall to meet with her parents.

Then it's just Fairy and me. We haven't been alone together since the night of the Formal. I instantly feel convicted of my actions over past month, and I want to vomit. Why is it that I always want to get sick around her?

"Hello, Arbor," Fairy speaks softly to me. I look at her and feel that bile rising up in me again. I want to leave.

"That girl," I say to her, "is amazing. Cinco deserves to be here and it would be a shame if she isn't. Maybe she can be the one to help you in the way..." I paused, fighting down the tears. "Maybe she can help you in the way I can't."

With that I rush past her before she can say anything. I make my way up to my room, taking the steps two at time. I can't do class today. I need to be alone. I hate this place and the way it makes my emotions overflow. I run to my room, open the door, throw all my stuff down, hop on my bed, and I release a month's worth of tears.

CHAPTER TWENTY

He's in my head again. I try not to go back down that road. I've been lying here all day trying to do everything but think of Patrick. If I'm not thinking of Patrick then I'm thinking of Flag, if not Flag then my mind goes to Fairy, and then Spring, and then Cinco. I just want to forget it all.

Goose comes and checks on me after I don't show up for English. I tell her that I'm sick and all I want to do is sleep. I see that she isn't quite sold but she leaves me alone nevertheless. She promises to check on me later and bring me some food. I go back to bed and try to escape my thoughts. Escape the guilt that's building in me. I'm crying again. Why can't I find the happiness that everyone wants for me? I hate crying. At this point, I don't think I will ever stop crying. I hate all of this. What have I done? Poor Flag. I can't believe I treated him that way. All he was trying to do was help me, which hurt the worst.

When I've pushed everyone away, trying to sabotage all relationships, here is this smart, funny, adorable boy still trying to help me and I trashed him. The image of his face after I said the words to him never leaves me. My mind is like a collage of pictures fragmented and put together in my head over and over again. I wish I could be something to them like they are to me. Spring, Columbus, Shadow... all of them. The only person I don't feel guilty over is Valentine and her bloody nose. She still deserves it, but I shouldn't have fought Fairy, shouldn't have stormed out of her office that night. I'm such a stubborn idiot. I don't even think idiot is the right word. Child. I acted like a child.

She sees something in me, something that only my parents ever saw and expressed to me that it was there. I feel the tears coming again, and I turn over to fight them with sleep. When I awake, it's dark outside. I have vague memories of Goose coming and bringing me some soup. Checking the clock, I see it's after one a.m. I risk a trip to the bathroom, and thankfully, no one else is out and about. When I get back to my room, I start gathering up the things that I chucked all over the place. As I'm picking up my bag and books, some papers slip out, and with them is the picture of Patrick and I that Flag gave me. I didn't even know that I took it. I glance up at the clock again and realize he may still be there. I need this guilt gone, I need to find out if there is any way I can build the bridges back. More than any fast-removed bandaged, this is going to hurt. Hurt badly.

I push myself up, check the mirror and see that my eyes look like someone battling an unexpected case of double pink eye. But this will have to do. I leave my room and make my way down to the lounge. I glance in and see that, yes, Patrick is there.

I open the door and it feels like that first night all over again. There he is, headphones in, deep in thought, and working hard. I battle the urge to leave right then. He wouldn't even know I had been there. I stand there for an hour or about five minutes, trying to decide the best way to approach him without scaring him to death again.

"I know you're there, Arbor," he says, not looking up, continuing to write. I smile to myself. Of course he knows I'm there. Now I'm thankful that I didn't back out and leave.

Patrick finishes writing whatever he is working on and takes the headphones out. I make my way over and sit across from him. Now that I'm here, I have no clue what I'm going to say. There are too many things that need to be said, so many things I need to apologize for, and that's when I realize what I should say. "I'm sorry, Patrick," I say quietly to him.

Then we sit. He doesn't say anything at first. I don't say anything. We just sit. I guess there really isn't anything else to say, so I take out the necklace he gave me and reach to give it back. "I don't deserve this," I tell him, setting it in front of him. "It should go to someone special, someone worthy of it."

I see him take the necklace and put his palm around it. He looks sad and pained. I remember that first night when he told me about how much he likes cooking and how he doesn't get to do it unless his grades are perfect. I ache remembering the closeness that we shared that night. But that was then, this is now. Patrick will move on and do great things. Next year maybe he will find someone to share the burden with. I can never be the person he deserves.

"Arbor," He says, looking at me with the green eyes that haunt my mind. "I did give this to someone special and worthy. This belongs to you and no one else." I see that his eyes are glistening and I panic that he's going to burst into tears. That's the last thing I need for him to do. If he starts crying I'm not going to be able to handle it at all. No, I won't let him. I stand up and do the boldest thing I can think of. I kiss him.

It happens before I can second-guess it. I cross over to him, take his face in my hands and kiss him. My first kiss. And it's terrible. I'm horrified. My mouth practically misses his mouth so I kind of half kiss his lips. I press too hard and I our noses are squished together. I don't know what to do with my tongue.

Do I open my mouth? Don't open my mouth? So I kind of end up dive bombing his mouth. How long is this supposed to last? Eyes closed the whole time?

Finally, thankfully, Patrick takes control and moves us apart.

"That was, um, unexpected," he says, looking at me utterly confused.

"Oh my goodness, I'm an idiot," I say, starting to back away and head back to the door.

"No, no, Arbor." He catches me by the door. "I'm not letting you get away that easy. Do you know how many nights I've waited for you to come back down here?" He guides me over to one of the couches and we sit down. He holds both my hands and we sit close to each other. I tell him all about Cinco and the excitement she has to get the chance to come to Holiday High. I tell him all about the fight with Fairy and how I yelled at Flag and how I've missed him so much and how I'm scared to death of the Confirmation and how I'm babbling on like Cinco. I must have talked for thirty minutes straight without him saying a word.

"Arbor, it's fine," he finally says to me. "It's okay. Everyone is okay. We all still love you." He catches himself. Love? "I meant, uh , I meant," he stumbles, turning beet red.

I start to laugh. It feels so good to laugh with Patrick. Like a sip of an elixir that I've been depriving myself of. He goes on to catch me up on how his parents don't want him go back to Ireland this summer and they are having a big fight about it. His father is threatening to pull him out of mentoring with Muffin if he goes back. I feel so sad, for him and for the fact that I haven't been there for him.

"Now, about that kiss earlier," he says, and it's my chance to turn red.

"Hey, I'm smooth," I tell him.

He starts to laugh at me, and I slap him playfully. I don't remember the last time I let myself be playful. It's foreign to me and I don't think it's something I deserve to do, not after the way I've been acting. I stop laughing and just sigh. Patrick asks me what's wrong.

"Will you forgive me, Patrick?" I ask. "I have been terrible. I really am sorry. I was just so mad; mad beyond anything I've ever been mad at before. This whole school, all of it, everything between Majors and Minors, the pressure to be something more than I've ever been, and when I saw Valentine trying to take away Spring's moment, I just snapped. I lost it. But none of that's your fault and I pushed you away." He takes my hand again and looks deep into me.

"I do forgive you, Arbor," he says to me. "But it's not just me that you need to talk to. It's not just me that you've pushed away. Spring, Flag, Santa, and everyone else at our table have been missing you. No one really knows what happened. Santa took the blame and said that an incident happened in mentoring and he was to blame."

I was speechless. I can't believe Santa did that, why would he do that?

"To keep the holidays together, of course." I could hear Fairy explaining it to me now. My stomach turns and twists back into that sick feeling again. This is why it's so easy to stay in the bitter, hating-the-world, pushing-everyone- away-world that I had created. It's going to take so much work and pain to tear down the walls I put up. For the first time in my life, I actually see my future in my eyes. I see myself grown up, living in the woods like my parents, amongst the trees and animals. I see myself traveling like them, trying to nurture the holiday to make it work like they do. Continuing to struggle to gain traction and a following. To get people to understand the true reason for celebrating our Day. But something is different with my future than theirs. I see myself alone.

The tears start falling down my cheeks again when I realize that I don't want that. Being alone isn't the future I want. I want to see myself with my friends, the other holidays, all working together to make each other's holidays the best they can be. I get it.

I finally understand what Fairy has been trying to show me all year. This divide can't continue to grow. If it does, then we're destined to be a country of a few big holidays. A country dominated by the celebration of shallow, petty, surface-only celebrations. Not the rich, thick, layered year of holidays the way it should be. We are all important. I'm important.

It doesn't matter if our holiday is the oldest, the newest, started here, celebrated at the beginning of the year, middle or end of the year and it doesn't matter if we're a Major or Minor. It matters that we're a holiday.

I look at my watch. It's 3 a.m., and I realize now that I don't want to be alone, starting right now. I say good night to Patrick. I thank him over and over and I apologize again and again. He puts the necklace around my neck and I'm afraid he's going to try and kiss me. I hope someday that happens, but not right now. I think I'm scarred for life when it comes to putting my lips on anything. But he doesn't, he just looks at me and smiles. He tells me again and again that it's alright.

I leave the Lounge and I run back up to my floor. I stop at the second door and pause. I look at the pastel colors decorating it and I smile. I hope she won't mind being woken up. I touch her plate that reads Daylight's Savings and I feel that sick feeling again. But this time I know that's the fear trying to defeat me, and I won't it let win. I take a deep breath and knock.

CHAPTER TWENTY-ONE

S tanding here waiting for Spring to answer the door is torture. I wait nervously as I hear her fumbling and mumbling around. I feel more prepared for this encounter than I did when going to see Patrick but it's not going to be fun. From day one Spring was the most welcoming and loving person I think I've ever met. It was a gift to me. I feel like I won the jackpot and then just gave it back. I shake my head. Who does that? Seriously, who would win the jackpot, the top prize, the best there is and then says, "No thank you. I'd rather not enjoy this. You can have it back."

I see the knob turn and the door opens. There stands Spring, black hair disheveled in all different directions, half asleep and wearing red pastel pajamas with green flowers. She's still rubbing her eyes when she finally sees that it's me. Then her eyes widen to the shape of saucers.

"Arbor!" She gasps. Before I can say a word she's pulled me inside her room and is hugging me tight. Too tight, actually. I have to pull away from her to get my breathing back. Spring is a world-champion hugger. I barely catch my breath when I'm pulled in for round two of the vice-gripped hug. When she finally lets me go, I'm already tearing up, which makes Spring just hug me again.

"Spring," I say, gasping for air again. "Please, no more hugs." We stand there staring at each other. Spring has the biggest smile on her face, tears already forming in her eyes. My water-filled eyes continue to flow as I take in my friend, the closest thing I've had to a sister. I'm such a fool. We curl up on Spring's red couch that's covered in pastel green pillows. I thought I was prepared, but now that the moment is here, I don't know where to begin.

"I'm sorry for waking you up," I say. It seemed the easiest thing to apologize for. Maybe I can start small and build to the bigger ones. Sorry for waking you up. Sorry for pushing you away and trying to ruin our friendship. You know, something like that.

"It's okay, Arbor," Spring says, grasping both of my hands. "You can wake me up anytime." And there they come again, the tears. I'm a blubbery newborn-needing-milk mess. I just shake my head in disbelief at how I put myself in this situation.

"Listen," I begin. "I'm sorry for everything." I spend the next hour telling Spring all about what led me to my isolation. Just like Patrick, she's more than willing to forgive me. In fact, she says that it's all forgotten and she even starts to apologize to me for giving up and not trying hard enough to break me out of my self-imposed prison. I just laugh at that. Of course Spring would be apologizing to me. This girl is so self-sacrificing.

By the time we finish, I'm drained and so I sleep on the couch in Spring's room. She wakes me up for the 7 a.m. morning ritual and I feel the dread come to me as I realize that now I have to face Columbus, Shadow, and the rest of our girls. As we enter the bathroom, Shadow is the only one there. She looks at me, back to Spring, then back to me.

"Are you back to normal?" she asks me. I smile and nod. "Good. Because you have been super annoying." And with that, she's back to getting ready. I love that girl. The rest of the girls were so loving and accepting that the main thing I felt was stupidity.

Why had I insisted on being like this? Again, I fight the tears as we get ready for the day and head downstairs.

As we enter the dining hall Patrick is serving the cereal muffins, and yes, you just add milk, and they are amazing. He greets me like nothing had ever changed. The girls start giggling like they know a secret. I just roll my eyes and we make our way to our table.

The boys are already there. Pres, Santa, Fourth with Pop, Fall, who is sleeping, and Flag. The awake ones look up in complete surprise to see me standing there with the rest of the crew. While the other girls take their seats, I remain standing which draws some curious looks. They all look at me confused, like maybe I'm going to stand and eat. I take a deep breath.

"I just want to say something," I start. "As of right now, I don't know if I deserve to sit here anymore. I've spent the last few weeks pushing everyone away and treating them as the source of my problems. I'm ashamed to say that even when one of you came to me, trying to bring me back to my happy ways, I treated him badly."

I notice Flag looking down. My heart aches and I can't imagine the hurt that I caused him. "Flag," I continue, "I'm so sorry for what I said and the way I treated you. I ask for your forgiveness and I know I don't deserve it. I totally understand if you don't want me to sit at your table." I see a smile start to twitch at the mention of it being his table.

"I'm very sorry, Flag, and to all of you." I finish and stand there awkwardly. Talking to Patrick and the girls was one thing. I didn't yell and insult them in front of the entire student body. I wouldn't blame Flag at all if he didn't want me to be near him right now. "I've been an incredible jerk to everyone. But I'm truly sorry and will only sit back here again if it's okay with Flag."

With that, I wait. I see Flag calculating in his head. "Arbor," he says in a serious tone. This is it. I did go too far. Of course I did. Why wouldn't I take my issues and problems and project them onto Flag? I feel more ashamed than I have ever felt. I deserve what is coming to me.

But surprisingly Flag breaks into a wide grin. "I told you," he says. "You weren't happy. But now you look happy. For the first time in a long time, you look like Arbor." He keeps grinning and looks at everyone else at the table. "I would love for you to sit with us again. Is everyone okay with that?"

"You're the boss, Applesauce," Pres says. We laugh and I sit down between Shadow and Columbus. I see Spring grinning for the duration of breakfast. I feel myself relaxing and breathing for the first time in weeks. I didn't even realize how much stress I was putting on myself with the self-imposed isolation.

At one point Fourth and Santa try to take a water bottle and flip it to land on its bottom. They misjudge terribly and it hits Fall in the head. He jolts up, looking around like crazy and his eyes land on me. "Okay," he says. Then the bell rings and we make our way to morning assembly.

I go throughout the rest of the day with what I'm assuming is a pep in my step. Class goes quickly, lunch is my favorite chicken Alfredo muffins, and in P.E., Coach takes it easy on us by letting us do yoga. It isn't until after P.E. that I feel the first sense of dread. Santa grabs my arm as we head into the locker rooms.

"Hey, Arbor," he says. "I'm so happy you're back to normal and all, but you know there is someone else you should probably talk to." I stare at him for a bit. Who is he talking about?

"You need to go see Fairy, Arbor," he says with the stone-jawed look he gives when he's being serious. His words stop me cold in my tracks. I haven't even thought about Fairy in the last 24 hours. Why is that? Santa is completely right. If there is any other fence that needs to be rebuilt, it's that one. I go through redressing in a daze, my mind thinking over all the possibilities that could happen when or if Fairy would meet with me. I cleared things with Reaper and made my way to Fairy's office. It would be an exaggeration to say that this is what a death row inmate would feel like, but it doesn't feel good. With each step, I feel my legs crumble, but it's something that needs to be done and I know it.

Fairy's door is ajar and light is coming from the inside. I entered her office with the final of what I hope is the last of these dreaded talks. Never again would I ever push people away like this. The aftermath is torture. While my friends have been more responsive than I ever could have imagined, I can't hope for the same from Fairy. She's not my peer, my equal.

But instead of finding Fairy sitting warmly behind her desk, I found the other last person I didn't want to see, Frost. He was just putting up some files in Fairy's cabinet when he turned and saw me entering. "Well," he said cold and slow. "You will tell me why YOU are here right now."

Those cold eyes seem to drill their ice into me. I never find myself more frozen with stillness than I'm in his presence. Especially now since I wasn't even expecting him. I didn't even have time to really ponder on why he was in Fairy's office. "Um," I stammered. "I need to speak with Fairy."

"It's my understanding that you're no longer being mentored by her." He asks me back. "So again, you will tell me why you're here." He crosses over in front of the desk, closing the gap and bringing the chill with him. "I just..." I continue on. "I just need to tell her something. That I'm sorry."

"You are sorry?" he questions me back. I kind of shuffle my way back towards the door, ready to make my exit. "It's okay," I start to say. "I can come back later."

"You will stay," he orders, and I freeze. HA. Freeze.

"You will come back over here and have a seat." He motions me to the chair that I've spent many days listening to Fairy. I slowly start to make my way over to sit down. I don't like being this close to Frost. Not only is it uncomfortably cold, but he just plain creeps me out. Why is he always so close to people?

"I really hope you're not here to make amends with our dear Fairy," he says to me. "You were just starting to be interesting to me." Well, if that wasn't all the motivation I needed to change my ways. "Tell me, Miss Day," his voice slithering. "Do you think that making good with Fairy and those OTHER holidays will really help you? You do realize that the Confirmation is upon us in just two weeks."

I did realize that the Confirmation was in two weeks. I've given no thought to it since I had no plans of returning to Holiday High next year. But to hear Frost claim that Fairy and the others would not help me makes a little fire start up in me. A fire that hadn't been there in a long time.

"But, Arbor," he says, moving even closer to me, making my breath turn to mist. "You can make much more of an impact, secure your future here, and make your parent's lives so much better if you choose to align with my mentees." He takes his finger and places it underneath my chin. I inwardly cringe at the feel of his clammy, cold touch.

"Don't waste your time with Fairy and her ways of leading the Council," he says, gently moving his finger around my ear and through my hair. "Your holiday can become a power. A Major."

"What is going on here?" I jump and turn to see Fairy and Santa standing in the doorway. Frost moves away quickly but not without making eye contact with me. The look conveys to me what I already know, "This stays between us."

"I was just returning the files that you loaned me the other day," Frost says, making his way past them. "Thank you again, it made for some interesting reading." With that, Frost and his chill depart. Fairy turns her attention to me. "So, Arbor," she says. "I hear you want to speak to me."

Chapter Twenty-Two

airy and Santa make their way over to take their seats—Santa in his normal seat, Fairy behind her desk. I'm still reeling from the unexpected Frost visit and feel unprepared for this talk. On top of that, Fairy looks extremely serious.

"Santa just came and found me to tell me that you wanted to visit," Fairy says, minus the normal warmth that she exudes. I find myself wishing to be back at my normal school. Not my normal longing. All of a sudden I have an intense longing for something normal. Anything that resembles what life at high school should be. Maybe a nice spelling bee? At this point, my life is so upside down that I would happily stand in front of a group of people and try to spell words.

"Arbor?" I hear Fairy ask.

"What is the country of origin?" I say to her, still lost in my thoughts.

"Excuse me?" she asks me quizzically. I snap out and try to refocus my brain on the task at hand. Even if Fairy isn't open to me anymore, I know I still need to try to make this right. I take a deep breath and launch into my apologetic ways again. Fairy takes this in calmly, not revealing her hand.

"Again, I should not have acted the way I did." I finish up and the silence in the room is heavy. I feel so tired.

I steal a glance at Santa, who gives a short nod. He has a steely look on his face that I can't quite read. Is he bracing for backlash? Is he ready to forgive and move on? I wish he would give some sort of sign.

"Well, Arbor, that's all well and good," Fairy says, finally cutting through the silence. "And I agree you should not have acted the way you did. It was uncalled for, an absolute disgrace to you, your family, and your holiday. While you have spent that last month or so acting like a child Santa and I have been working hard trying to mend the hurt that you have caused all while still continuing the progress to bring the holidays together. Which, I might add, that your stunt and attitude has not helped us in that endeavor."

I sink my head and listen. I have no defense because she's right. I let my temper overtake me the night of the Formal and since then I've had childish behavior. I feel sickness start to bubble in my stomach. I know that sitting here is where I need to be, where I WANT to be right now but now the side effects of all of the stress of reconciliation are hitting me. Tired, drained, exhausted. No matter how I put it, I'm just finished. It dawns on me that all one can do is simply accept responsibility for their actions, commit to the road of sorry, and hope for the best. If the returning party won't accept, then you can't force them.

All I've I wanted was to be released from Holiday High and this world. It seems like that wish will be granted. "While this behavior of yours isn't acceptable," Fairy carries on. "Look at me, Arbor." I raise my eyes to meet hers. "It's not acceptable at all. Do you understand that now?" she asks me.

"I do," I offer. I almost start to go on again about everything I did and all I messed up. I realize that this is the point where I put that behind and I move forward. I do truly understand what I did.

My actions can still control me again. This time letting the guilt be carried around like chains.

"I'm glad to hear that," she continues, leaning forward on her desk. "To be honest, Arbor, and I do adore honesty. I'm not sure that you're ready for what is needed. Perhaps that's my mistake." Fairy sighs and for the first time, I see how tired she looks. I fight the urge again to let my guilt overcome me. "Press on towards better things," I can hear my father saying to me.

"Perhaps I put too much pressure on you, allowing you to see into my world and it's probably too soon. My goodness, Arbor. The first day you were here, I was telling the sad affairs of the Holiday Council." Fairy pinches her nose and lowers her head a little.

"Maybe keeping you with Reaper is the proper thing to do now," she sighs. "My inclination is to do that. Especially with the Confirmation so close." Her eyes open and I see the motherly gaze that I've come to know.

"But, Arbor," She says softly. "You're special. I'm sorry you were here alone with Frost, but Santa came and found me as soon as your class with Coach Bunyan was finished. He told me about the Arbor he saw today. The one that was humble, fearful, and sorrowful. It doesn't take as much strength to let anger control a person. It takes more strength to seek to right a wrong. Humility hurts. It cuts deep. Santa says he still believes in you. That the other Majors in your life believe in you." She stops. I glance at Santa, who is now looking down and away from me.

"Is that true?" I say barely over a whisper. I see his face soften and his shoulders relax. He offers me a soft smile. "Of course it is," Santa begins. "As soon as I saw you walk in this morning, I breathed a huge sigh of relief. I can't do this without you. I don't want to do this without you. I don't see things the way you do. I've been in this world for too long." I take in his words like an elixir. I feel energy from them.

"One more thing, Arbor," Santa offers. "And I'm very serious when I say this." He sits up straight. He looks at me. I feel uncomfortable, but by his gaze I know he means business.

"You need to start believing in yourself," he states, not breaking the gaze. "From this point on, no more talk of 'I can't do this.' No more, 'I haven't been here long enough.' From this point, no more doubt. We believe in you and now it's time for you to stop that excuse and embrace this."

When he's finished, he lets out a big breath and relaxes but still never breaking eye contact. I get a glimpse in my mind I see him as the leader he was born to be. The leader of the holidays. I see him older, distinguished. It makes me proud. Proud that he's the future of us.

"Well said, Santa," Fairy says, breaking the silence. We all three sit in silence for a minute. I try to configure in my head the proper response to all of this. Fairy is doubting me, Santa believes in me, and Frost wants me to join him. But at this moment it's the only thing that matters to me and that's the reason I came to this office.

"I can only hope that you will once again find that belief in me," I say to Fairy, trying my best to come across as confident. "Regardless of what happens with my future at Holiday High, I need you to know that I am sincerely sorry for my actions. Both with hitting Valentine and my actions afterward. I let my frustrations get the best of me."

I see a smile come across Fairy's face and I relax some. The glow that had disappeared returns behind her and a warmth comes across me. Oh, how I missed the comfort of this room with these two people.

"I understand Arbor," Fairy says. "Valentine can, um, be a bit of a challenge at times."

Santa actually lets out a laugh and we all smile. "I will speak with Reaper and see if he's willing to let you come back to my mentoring hour. That's unless you would rather stay with him?"

"Or with Frost?" Santa offers with a sly smile.

"I'm fine right where I am. Here with you both."

CHAPTER TWENTY-THREE

The next two weeks leading up to the Confirmation is a whirlwind. The tension level has risen to new heights as all Minor holidays prepare to face the Holiday Council. Even Spring isn't immune to the stress. I'm in the middle of enjoying my fried chicken muffin, trying to actually forget about the Confirmation when Spring starts rushing us all to finish. "Eat faster!" Spring cries. "We need to get to the lounge right away." The glance she gives us Minors isn't the same friendly, motherly Spring. That Spring has been replaced with another Spring. A crazy Spring. "You are going to do fine," Santa says, rubbing her shoulders. "Just relax. Let people eat their dinner."

"DINNER??!" Spring shrieks. "How can we be concerned with dinner? The future of our holiday depends on how we do next week. I present first on Monday. Today is Friday. Tomorrow is Saturday. Then Sunday. Then it's Monday. Then I'm presenting. Oh my goodness!" She continues slapping the table, startling everyone and even waking up Fall. "Eat faster!" "What is happening?" Fall says, half awake. "Your sister is freaking out about Confirmation," April answers him. "Oh...so normal," says Fall, laying his head back down.

Outwardly I may not be in the same frantic state as Spring, but inwardly I'm feeling the pressure all the same. I was scheduled to give my presentation last. The very last person to speak. It's complete torture. I have to sit through four days of presentations before they get to Thursday afternoon. I would much rather be like Spring and present first on Monday morning. Then it's over. Finished, and whatever the outcome, I can get it over with.

The only advantage to presenting in my spot is I have extra time to work with Fairy. Not a day goes by when I don't kick myself for losing time with her. Valuable time has been lost.

We spend the whole time in mentoring preparing for my presentation. Santa has proved to be amazing. While he doesn't know the pressure of the Confirmation, he does know how the Holiday Council thinks.

"They want to see that you have matured over this year," he says to me again. "Trust me when I say that they all know about the incident at the Formal. This is your chance to show them that it was an isolated incident. That it's not who Arbor really is."

I groan inwardly at his words. Wishing for the millionth time that I could go back in time and tell myself not to lose my cool. I silently scold myself again for putting myself in this position. "Bad Arbor." "So who you are," he continues. "Be honest with them. Don't be afraid to tell them your whole journey here. From the first doubting moments to now. Own up to your mistakes, don't beat around the bush. Be polite." I stifled a laugh and he looked at me funny.

"You want me to talk about how much I didn't want to come here, how I had to drag my concrete feet up the steps. How I think the Holiday Council stands for everything that's wrong with our holiday. And you want me to be polite in doing it?"

Santa pauses for a second and gets a thoughtful look on his face. "Well maybe you can be a little less Arborish?" he offers. I sigh and smile at him. "You bet." That night I decide to spend my time preparing in my room. Which didn't sit well with Spring. Apparently my presence in the study lounge was essential to her.

"You can't stay up here, Arbor!" Spring cries. "You will throw off my entire groove. You sit with me, you sit to the right, Patrick across from you, Santa beside me. The next table holds Flag, Pres, Columbus, and Shadow. Everything has to be the same. Same group. Same spots. Same temperature. Same time. All the same."

I sit wide-eyed staring at Spring. Columbus and Shadow, too, sit there staring at this obsessed monster in front of us. Spring slowly starts to catch her breath and regain her composure.

"I will be okay," she says, mainly to herself. "I will be okay. It's okay if Arbor isn't there. She has her room, she can stay. Why shouldn't she? It's a nice room, a great room, maybe I should stay here, too. Who knows? It may help. Shadow hops up and starts leading Spring to the door.

"I think this is a good time for us to leave," Shadow says calmly. Spring keeps muttering as Shadow and Columbus guide her out. Columbus pauses before leaving. "You can do it, kid!" she yells and laughs on the way out. Always the coach. Finally the silence. I put my buds in and start to relax to the sounds of the latest Korean boy band I've found, and I get lost in my thoughts on the Confirmation. Be honest. Be polite. Be original. Be strong.

Why is my holiday important? What sets it apart from the other holidays? What does the future hold for Arbor Day? I continued to think and brainstorm, still feeling like I was getting nowhere. I tried all the tricks I could think of. I set a timer for 30 minutes and wrote nonstop. I just let my mind wander and see what happened. I looked back on it and am pretty certain that my holiday has nothing to do with being one inch tall. I think of acronyms for T.R.E.E. Trees Really Excel Earth. The Right Earth Evolves. Tiny Robots Eat Earthlings. Yeah, those don't work either.

Finally, I close my notebook in disgust. I couldn't stomach anymore. Besides, I was downing coffee like crazy. I needed a break, so I headed to the bathroom. I grabbed my shower stuff because I read somewhere that good ideas come in the shower.

CHAPTER TWENTY-FOUR

ll my time over the next few days is consumed with my presentation, which doesn't leave much time for my studies. Say what you will about Holiday High, but the sheer fact that they don't "believe in finals" might make it the best school on the planet. I can't even imagine preparing for this Confirmation on top of studying.

I spend Friday night imprisoned with the others in the study lounge. Flag and Pres are fretting over what suit Pres should wear for his speech while Columbus is talking Spring down off another ledge of panic. Across from me, April is trying hard to keep Fall awake enough to work on his presentation. It's getting close to midnight when Patrick, Shadow, and Santa enter the room.

"Okay, guys, enough is enough," Santa announces. I look up to see our three Major friends dressed in what can only be described as stuffed animals meet warriors. They all have weird looking furry hats on their heads with war paint on their faces. I have no clue what they are up to but it has to be better than spending another late night in the study lounge.

"Seriously, guys. Enough is enough," Shadow says, dressed in an Animée kimono with black streaks across her face. "Get up and let's go."

We all kind of stare at each other trying to figure out what in the world these three Majors have in store for us. I see Flag and Pres quickly start to pack everything up, seemingly scared of Shadow. I can't blame them.

I, too, start to put everything away. I feel exhausted and would rather be headed to bed but the sight of Patrick wearing furry green bunny ears and a golden suit makes me so intrigued. I notice April start to shake Fall awake and explain to us that we're requested to leave when Fall's eyes get really big.

"Why is Santa dressed like a sunburned polar bear?" He says. I'm sure that sentence has never been uttered anywhere else in the history of time. April starts to drag Fall up from the table. "Seriously," Fall keeps on saying. "Am I dreaming?"

"SLIDES!"

We all stop at the shout coming from across the room where Columbus is desperately trying to drag Spring up from her work. "MY SLIDES! MY SLIDES!" Spring is screaming. "I need to get this presentation perfect."

I chuckle to myself as Columbus is dragging Spring feet first away from the table. Santa marches over and picks up Spring and throws her over his shoulder as we all make our way out into the hallway. "MY SLIDES!" Spring screams as the door shuts behind us.

We make our way down the hall to the foyer when Santa finally decides to put Spring down. After which she promptly makes an about-face and heads back towards the study lounge.

"Oh, no you don't," Santa says scooping her back up on his shoulders. "But my slides," she says in protest.

We all ignore her stress and make our way out back following our three uniquely dressed leaders. We're headed down the east side hill which I find strange because the only thing back here is the shed where Coach Bunyan houses all the sports equipment.

As we make our way down I can't help but think about what has brought all these people together. Spring and Pres welcoming me in my first class. Shadow and Columbus being the great girls that they are to welcome me to eat with them. April breaking herself away from Valentine and finding someone that loves and accepts her like Fall does. Laughing as I remember Fall sleeping....well sleeping everywhere. Then there is Flag. The youngest in the school. The smartest in the school. My heart still aches and I remember back to my rudeness towards him. Then there is Patrick.

My mind goes back to that first night in the study lounge. That first night when I entered, expecting to be alone. But instead, Patrick was seated, headphones in, and studying hard.

But before I can get lost in the moment, I'm interrupted by Shadow's announcement that we have arrived. I snap out of the memory and see that sure enough we have ended our trek at the storage shed. It looks dark and locked up.

"Before we enter," Santa explains as he sets Spring down on the ground and Columbus takes up the guard on her. "You need to look through our boxes here and pick some outfits."

"Is there a suit?" Pres asks. Shadow makes her way over to him, takes him by the shoulders, and looks into his eyes.

"Pres," She says. "For once you don't have to wear a suit. Do you sleep in a suit?" Before he can answer, Spring tries to make a run for it. Before she gets two steps away, Columbus has her by the waist.

"No, you don't," she says, dropping Spring back down.

"But my slides!"

"NO ONE CARES ABOUT YOUR SLIDES!" We all yell at once. Which makes Spring seems a little frightened but then she starts to laugh. And I do mean laugh. She laughs like she hasn't laughed in years.

"Great," Columbus utters. "She's finally cracked."

"Slides! Slides! It's all about the slides," Spring says laughing. When she finally calms down she stands up and shakes like a dog out of a bath. "I'm fine," she announces. When no one moves and just stares at her, she assures again. "Really, I'm okay."

"Now, if I can have all of your attention, please." I turn to see Patrick standing in front of a big red and green box I recognize from Grimm and the theater department. Patrick, Santa, and Shadow all take positions by the crate and lift the lid off.

"Everyone come on up and find an outfit," Shadow says. "None of you're going in there unless you're dressed for fun." She starts pulling items out of the box hat. All the things are a mix of the red and green colors of Holiday High. She grabs a big green sombrero and tosses it to Pres. "Here you go. This is your style."

Pres pauses for a second, then shrugs and puts it on. Shadow invites the others to start digging through the stuff. I see Spring squeal when she pulls out a fancy red dress that looks like something a fancy princess would wear. Santa helps her slip it on and then tops her off with a green afro wig. Too bad she won't have a picture of this in her slides.

Just then, I notice Patrick making his way over to me. He is holding something red and he has a sly smile on his face. "I don't know what you're holding but that look tells me it's not something I would have picked out." I laugh at him.

"What?" Patrick says cocking his head to the side. "You don't trust me?" When he reaches me, he starts to unfold the furry red thing. My eyes bug out of my head.

"No," I say sternly. "No way in the world." Being held in Patrick's hands in a giant heart. The heart has holes placed in exactly where my head, arms, and legs come out. Written in cursive on the front of the heart are the words "Be my Valentine." I throw up a little in my mouth at the sight of it.

"Come on!" Patrick says, giving that sly smile again. "Where is your sense of humor?"

"I would rather go in there naked than wear that," I snap back.

"Oh really?" He says, raising his eyebrows.

"You wish," I say, pushing by him toward the giant box. I start digging through the massive amount of clothes, wigs, and costumes. I see a dog head, an Elvis outfit, and other items that would make anyone embarrassed to wear. Finally, down at the bottom, I see something and a giant smile spreads across my face.

"You wanna see my sense of humor, Patrick?" I say, keeping my back to him. I put on the outfit and then turn to reveal my choice. It's Patrick's eyes that bug out now.

"No," He says sternly. "No way in the world."

"Too late," I laugh at him. I grin as I see him take in the sight of me standing in front of him in a giant shamrock with musical notes all over it and giant letters that say, "SHAMROCK N ROLL". I twisted and I turned showing it off to him and giving him my best model face. Patrick continues to just stare at me with an empty look.

"You have insulted my entire holiday," He deadpans. I laugh and throw my arms in the air. "SHAMROCK N ROLL!" I yell jumping up and down. With that, he can no longer hold it in and joins me in the laughter. It feels good. I realize that for five whole minutes, I have actually forgotten about the Confirmation and the fact that the whole future of my holiday is riding on my shoulders.

As our laughter continues, I hear a low groan start to grow from inside the shed. It grows and grows until I can actually feel it. Like when your stomach drops from going over a short hill in the car, it starts in my chest and drops into my gut. I see lights start to twirl and circle escape from the shed windows.

"Alright, everyone, let's get this party started." I escape my gut and see Santa addressing us all in front of the shed door. I take in the scene around me. All dressed up we look like a party store threw up all over us. But for the first time in weeks, we don't look stressed or worried. Even Spring has seemed to have forgotten her precious slides. Of course, her presentation would be deemed ridiculous if she were to present it wearing her current unicorn meets teddy bear outfit.

"Only one rule," Santa continues. "Once we're in here, there is no mention of school, mention of work, and no Confirmation talk. Just let loose and let it go."

With that, he opens the door and we file in. "Come on, Arbor," Patrick says, taking my hand. "It's time to Shamrock N Roll."

CHAPTER TWENTY-FIVE

A ll the supplies from the shed have been shoved to one side and some drinks have been set up on the other side. Of course, this is all hard to see as I've entered into a blinding circus of nonstop lights shooting in every direction possible.

The shed isn't very big but with a group this small we could have had plenty of room to be comfortable. The unfortunate thing now is that there is a stage setup taking up half the space. Upon it is a large turn table and speakers the size of refrigerators. The lights are erected all on top of the stage, the side of the stage, in the speakers, in the turntable, and even in the floor.

"YO! YO! YO! DJ Pauly B in the house!" Shouts Coach Bunyan. He is standing behind the table holding a microphone glittering with sparkles. Now we may have all been dressed up in crazy party store barf, but we're nothing compared to Coach.

Hair slicked back, wearing a Holiday High tracksuit with giant gold chains hanging off his neck. The top part of the tracksuit is unbuttoned, revealing a squirrel nest of chest hair. I swallow hard and I take in the best part of this outfit....bright pink fluffy headphones. He sets off an air horn that makes everyone grab their ears while he screams at us again.

"It's time to RAAAAAAAVE!"

Just then, a large siren erupts from the speakers, and music starts to pump. The lights and music start to pulse together at a crazy rate, and "DJ Pauly B" starts pumping his fist.

Before I know it Shadow, of all people, starts jumping up and down. She's throwing her hands in the air and turning around with the music. I see Columbus grab a giant bag and start handing out all kinds of contraptions to us. I don't really understand what is happening until I start to see lights coming from everyone. They are glow sticks! Not just sticks but bracelets, necklaces, cat ears, and glasses too. She finally throws the rest in the air and starts jumping around Shadow.

Patrick screams something at me, but I can't understand or hear him. Before I can figure it out, he drags me out into the crowded space and we join the others. I find myself entranced with the others. I'm swinging my glow sticks around, matching them to the rhythm of the music. It's enthralling. The closeness of the bodies, the feel of the bass, and the loudness of the music attach us all and make one musical organism.

I don't know how long this lasts, but finally, the glow starts to dim and Coach starts slowing the music down and people start to head towards the drinks. I suddenly find myself left on the floor with just Patrick and Shadow. Shadow is lost in her own world. Turning and twisting while moving her arms around. I suddenly get a glimpse of her dancing in a Native American drum circle.

"Now that's someone who dances to her own drummer," Patrick says to me. I nod in agreement and smile as I take in my friend. "Do you want something to drink?" Patrick asks me.

"Not right now," I answer back. "Let's just enjoy the space for a while."

"Hmmm." He smiles. "I don't think being closer is better." He pulls me closer and places his hands on my hips. I place my wrists around his neck and let out a short giggle. "What is so funny?"

"Nothing, " I answer. "I just realized that this is my first ever slow dance. It's not as awkward as it looked like in junior high."

"Well. I guess that's good. I would hate to think that being this close to me would be so awkward." He smiles that smile at me again, and I feel like I can't breathe all over again. My world starts to slow down again. The lights slow, the music drains and everything is moving in sync with just Patrick and me.

I feel the swell in my chest as I look into his green eyes. How can it be that I've looked into these eyes so many times but now feels like the first time I'm seeing them? Here goes everything.

I lean up to him quickly and plant my lips on his. I feel the surprise as he jerks slightly back, clearly not expecting this move. His body starts to relax and his lips gently press back on mine. I let go of this bliss and dare a look at him. His eyes are still closed but there is a sliver of smile on his face.

"Hey, guys!!" The moment is burst as Spring jumps beside us. "My slides! Can you believe I was so worried about something so —wait! Did you guys just kiss?"

I feel the heat come into my cheeks and I look at Spring standing there wide-eyed with her mouth hanging open. Before I can even start to say something, she's already tearing up and flapping her hands. "Aww!!" she squeals. "Aww! My little Arbor."

She busts Patrick and me apart, engulfing me in a giant hug. I lose my breath and look at Patrick for help.

"I think I will get us some drinks," he says, leaving me alone to die in the elephant embrace of Spring. She finally releases the vice. She then just stands there, her stare glowing at me.

"So," I say, "How about your slides?"

"Oh no, Arbor Day," she speaks to me. "We ARE going to talk about this."

"If I told you I would rather do anything else in the world right now, would that make a difference to you?

"Absolutely not." But before I can say anything, everything just dies. It's total blackness. The music is gone, the lights are gone. It feels like we have been sucked into a hole. It seems to last for hours or thirty seconds as the shed door busts open and a cold figure looms in its doorway. Frost, The shed lights come on and we're all frozen. Pun Intended.

Frost scans our faces. He notices that Shadow is still silently dancing in her world. "YOU!" he barks "You will stop that ludicrous movement right now."

I swear the moment he speaks it Shadow freezes with us. If I didn't know better, I would believe that Frost actually has some sort of supernatural force.

"You will all leave right now," he says in the slow, dark, cold way of his. "You will get those abominable costumes off and return to your rooms in exactly three minutes." I let out a short laugh and I instantly realize what happend.

"You will tell me what you think is so funny, Ms. Day," he says as those cold eyes lock on to me. Oh my goodness, what did I just do? Did I really just do that? The vice principal just ruined our rave and is clearly not pleased with us. And I just laughed? I'm truly the dumbest person alive. "You will speak now," he drawls out again.

"Um...." I stammer. I look around at my classmates their faces are filled with the same dread that I'm feeling. Even Coach has taken his fuzzy headphones off, awaiting my explanation.

"Um..., " I start again. "You said abominable, you know, like the snowman...cold...like frost...." I stop speaking. The look on Frost's face is damning. "You will all leave now!" Frost snaps, and I shut my eyes at the pierce of his tone. I let the chill of his words evaporate and I open my eyes again to face Frost alone.

But I'm not alone. None of my friends have moved. They are still standing right where they were when Frost entered. "You will all listen to me now. You will leave Ms. Day and I here." Frost says, looking around the room. "You WILL go. Now."

I can almost feel the icicles forming around the room. The slow cold that has seemed to suck all the warmth and glow out of the room. It doesn't seem possible that minutes ago we were all packed in here like sardines sweating with the music. My friends need to move now.

But no one moves. Not one inch. Maybe Frost has actually frozen them. "With all due respect, I think we will stay right here." It's Patrick who speaks up at my side.

"Yes," Spring chimes in. "I feel like this is the exact place I need to be right now." She links her arm into mine. I have never loved this girl more than I do right now.

"Even I'm going to stay awake for this," Fall speaks.

Frost stands there and I wonder for a second if ice is going to explode out of his ears. When most people turn red from anger, he seems to be turning a darker and colder blue. "You will regret this. Each of you," he exclaims to us. "For some of you," he says, looking right into my eyes. "You will not be back here next year." With that, he turns slowly and exits the shed.

Chapter Twenty-Six

It's Confirmation week. That's the first thought that greets me Monday morning as I wake up. It shocks me actually because I didn't think I even fell asleep. The whole night was spent working on my presentation with Spring. I roll over and take in my room. Sure enough, Spring is curled up on the floor staring blankly at some papers she's holding. It looks like she's actually....um, sleep reading? Is that a thing?

I check the clock and it says 11 a.m. Wow. Good thing classes are canceled in preparation for the events that evening. Every night this week different Minor holiday students will present to the council, faculty, and guests that will be in attendance. As it is, Spring is first tonight, and I'm last on Thursday night.

"You dead?" I try to say to Spring but it only comes out as a garbled mess of sounds. I clear my throat and try to find some strength.

"Are you alive, Spring?" I managed to say. I wait to see any response and finally, a hand slowly lifts up with a small thumbs up. Besides that movement, there really is no way to tell if she's really alive. She's surrounded by all the papers, note cards, and props of her presentation. Poor girl is using her backpack as a pillow. But before I can dwell on her too much it hits me that I only have until Friday to get my presentation finalized.

Ugh. Why did I ever climb those steps into this school? Why did I ever let my parents talk me into this? I can never get out of this bed since I'm held down by the weight of all of this. Not only will, I never be allowed back into Holiday High but I could set our holiday back to the Stone Age. All the work that I've seen my parents do during my 15 years can be undone by one speech. Yes, I do believe I will sleep all day.

"You can't stay in bed all day and sleep," a voice says to me.

"Is that you God?" I call out. "Am I doomed to this? Woe is me."

"It's not God," the voice says. " It's worse. It is I, Spring Forward!"

"Ugh! That *is* worse!" I say. Seconds later a notebook hits me and I start laughing. Spring crawls over to the bed and sits on her knees facing me.

"You will do great, Arbor," she offers. "I can't think of anyone else that I would want to have represent my holiday besides you. No one this year has grown as much as you or faced the pressure you have faced. You've got this."

I ponder on what Springs says and think again how blessed I am to have her. Maybe she's right. There is no way that the girl who climbed those steps could stand and present what I'm about to present in five days. I don't even recognize that girl. Distant, jaded, bitter, lonely, deprived of friends, love, and family.

"Well neither of us is going to be able to present anything if we don't get some food," I tell her. But before I sit up, I take her and look her in the eyes and pause for a moment.

"Thank you for that, Spring," I say. "And for everything this year. Your holiday is lucky to have you, too. It's all going to be downhill after your presentation today. No one can top you." I see the tears coming instantly.

'No, no, no, no, not today dear." I say as I quickly jump up. "No crying today. Let's get you cleaned up and get some food."

We make ourselves look presentable (pun intended) and make our way to see what Muffin has cooked up for us. We are making our way down the hall when we pass by Valentine's room. The door is cracked open and we hear her addressing her followers.

"I'm telling you," she's saying. Spring and I both stop. Instantly something tells my brain that I should keep moving on but I don't.

"She doesn't stand a chance," she continues. "No matter what kind of presentation she comes up with, no matter what kind of backing she gets from Fairy or the other teachers, Arbor will not be back next year."

I can't move. My stomach starts to flip flop and I break into a cold sweat. I start to reach for the door. I have to find out what she means. I must find out. What could Valentine know about me? Why is she saying that I won't be back here next year, and why is she so confident saying it?

Spring pulls me away from the door and drags me down the hall. We head down the stairs. Spring is trying to be encouraging but I'm in a catatonic state. Numb. What does Valentine know?

"HEY!" Spring is now yelling at me and shaking my shoulders. "Don't make me slap you because I will!" I slowly come around and make eye contact with her.

"There you are," Spring says. "If for a second you start to believe what that vile Valentine is spouting then you need to stop right now. She doesn't know anything. She has no power over you or the Confirmation.....do you hear me Arbor?" I do hear her. I mean the words are coming out of her mouth and going into my ears but they are not hitting their mark.

Valentine sounded so confident. So sure of herself. "I think I need to be alone for a bit," I stammer. I pull myself away and head off. I don't know where I'm really going until I find myself down the faculty hallway. I don't know if I'm purposely headed there but I find myself standing outside of Frost's office. I already feel the chill coming from the room. I move to knock, but stop myself. What good could come from talking to him?

"Hmmmm...." comes a voice behind me. "You've come to see me, Ms. Day?"

CHAPTER TWENTY-SEVEN

I turn around slowly. Frost is standing ever so close to me. Uncomfortably close. "You will come in now," he orders me. He slides by me and uses a long key tied on a string to open his office. He steps into the dark office. I, on the other hand, don't move. I'm not about to enter a dark, cold place with Frost.

"You will enter NOW," his voice comes from the darkness. I shuffle my feet and go into the cold. A small blue light flicks on from the desk and Frost has made it to his dark blue chair. "You will shut the door," He drawls and I comply.

"You will sit," and I take a seat on a blue metal chair. I gasp as I sit. The chair is freezing. I look around and take in Frost's office. Well, what there is to take in. Dark blue walls with nothing on them, the carpet the same color is under my feet. There is nothing on his desk. No phone, no computer, no notebook. Nothing. He has one file cabinet in the back corner but that's the entire contents of the room. Desk, his chair, my ice chair, a lamp, and that cabinet.

"I don't see the need for frivolous items in my office," he says taking notice of my wondering eyes. "If someone needs me, they can come to me. If I need someone, I can go to them. This place is mine. No one intrudes on it and no one is to be knocking on my door. Especially a student. Especially you."

I blow on my hands and shiver as he's addressing me. Any shock that I was feeling from Valentine's words is now replaced by fear. And the cold. Real cold. "So, Ms. Day," Frost says looking at me, his slow slithering way of speaking stopping my breathing. "Why were you at my door? And why were YOU about to knock on my door?." Now that's a good question.

"I...I..." I stutter. "I'm not very sure." Why was I there? Did my subconscious guide me here? Frost lets out a slow, low laugh. "I guess I wanted to ask you about something I heard today," I finally say. If anything to stop that laugh.

"And what would that question be?" he asks. If I've learned anything this year it's that I should think before I speak or act. I take a moment to decide exactly how to word this to Frost.

"I was wondering if you had any advice for my Confirmation presentation." Frost looks genuinely surprised.

"Hmmm," he says. "Do I have any advice for you?" he pauses. Bringing his hands up to his face like he's in prayer, I see the wheels turning in his mind. A smile comes across his face. Just a small short one, but I now notice it anyway. "Ms. Day."

Long pause. The longest pause. I don't think this room can get colder, but the temperature drops more. It feels like when you're caught outside right when a cold front moves in and finally over- takes the warmth.

"There is no advice to give you," Frost finally speaks. "There is no advice because there is nothing *to* you. You have shown nothing this year that would make me or anyone believe that you belong here or that you can handle the responsibilities of your holiday."

Frost's smile returns. This time in full view. He starts to speak again but after that smile, something in me stirs.

"No," I say, interrupting him. For the second time in this meet- ing, Frost is taken off guard.

"What gives you the right to speak when—"

"*NO!*" I say again louder. Well, that hits a mark. I see Frost's face turn a deeper shade of cold and his eyes grow smaller. "You're wrong," I say with way more strength than I'm feeling.

"I'm wrong?" Frost counters. "Please tell me how."

"Have you ever seen trees in the winter?" I ask him. I chuckle and move on before he can answer. "Of course you have," I say. "You love all things cold."

The laughing is helping to relax and unthaw me. "The one thing that's fascinating about trees in the winter is their branches." I continue on. "When the snow and frost and the ice hit the branches, they react to take care of the tree as a whole. The branches are bending and hanging low because of the stress. They are doing their job. They bend to let the heaviness slide off so the tree as a whole can survive. They always bend BUT they don't break. *I* will not be broken. Not by you, not by this school," I say with as much power as I can manage.

'You will see," I say, standing. "Bend but not break. I'm going to simply let you and the others slide off me." Frost starts to respond but I don't let him. "You will now be quiet."

With that, I turn around and leave.

I make it back to the warmth of the hall. I instantly feel like I could stand there for hours and let the cold slip away but I need to put Frost and his words behind me. I take the anger I'm feeling and make my way to the dining hall. My table is still filled with my friends and their gazes snap in my direction as soon as I enter. I grab my omelet muffin and head to the table.

I slam my tray down making everyone jump back and Fall snap awake.

"You okay, Arbor?" Columbus asks me.

"I'm better than okay," I answer, planting myself in the chair. "Friday can't come soon enough. This Confirmation is mine."

Chapter Twenty-Eight

The rest of the day moves quickly. I join the others as we decorate the auditorium for the first night of the Confirmation. With so many guests coming this week we spend all day raising banners, placing chairs on the stage, and dragging in a new podium for the event. I'm so glad my parents are only coming for Friday night. This is so over the top. Hanging above the stage is a giant red and green banner reading, "CONFIRMATION."

We have had to attach streamers to all the lights. Green and red bows adorn the seats. It's a spectacle. I've heard of a red carpet but we have taken it to a whole new level here. The red carpet is leading everywhere. I guess people feel more special walking a red carpet? Even to the bathrooms. Either that or people get lost easily.

We are sent upstairs in the late afternoon. I enter my room and see that my confirmation outfit has been dropped off. For the only time since I've been here, we all are to dress in the same formal outfit. While we all have different daily outfits that cater to us and we can accessorize, not so for the Confirmation. I unzip the bag and almost gag at the sight of it. For the Confirmation we have what I would assume is a more traditional school outfit. Long sleeve red shirt, with a green vest to go over it. The Holiday High logo is etched on the breast pocket. The next touch is a red and green checkered skirt of a, thankfully, tasteful length. Finally, my outfit seems to be complete with green knee-high socks with red sparkly dress shoes. Yes. Red sparkly dress shoes. I guess there is no place like Holiday High.

I get dressed and mock myself in the mirror. I go downstairs to the auditorium. I join Columbus and Shadow in line and Shadow looks like she could murder someone. "Why are you so upset?" I ask. "You're a Major, you don't even have to do the Confirmation." She shoots daggers at me.

"Do you see what I'm wearing?" She bites back. "This is everything wrong with the world."

"Yeah, everything," Columbus says. "Floods, genocide, diseases, death, and damnation but by all means this outfit is what's wrong with the world."

I can't help but laugh at this. It gets even funnier when Shadow turns the darkest shade of red. "Look!" Columbus exclaims. "Your face matches your outfit!" I laugh even more as Shadow gives us an "UMPF!" And heads away. Columbus and I are still laughing as we enter the hall with all the other students.

As I enter I do admit that we did a great job. The room takes my breath away. It's no longer the cold and stale room that we meet in every morning. It has been transformed. The streamers give off a bright glow of red and green while the whole room seems to be swimming in the school colors. We all take our seats. I notice right away that Santa's father is on the stage. The ACTUAL Santa is here. Now it's not the fantasy story of the guy delivering presents in one night but it's the man whose whole job is to make sure Christmas joy and cheer is spread. Seated by him must be Valentine's mother. Not only because I know she's on the Council but also because she's basically her daughter's twin. Just an older version. I make a mental note to never tell her that. The rest of the on-stage guests include Patrick's dad who is dressed in his Irish best, and Shadow's father, who, just like his daughter, has forgone all sense of formality and is dressed in what I can only describe as a parka meets muumuu.

The lights go dim and Coach Bunyan heads to the podium. Thankfully he has decided to forgo any crazy antics and is dressed in a nice dark green suit. "Are you FIRED UP!?" He yells into the crowd. Well, so much for no crazy antics. "Who is FIRED UP?"

No one moves. You can still hear his final UP ringing throughout the hall. If Coach notices, he doesn't let on. "Let's get FIRED UP!" he continues. "It's Confirmation week!" Now that does get a polite round of applause from the crowd. "That's what I'm talking about!" Coach yells. You have to admire his dedication.

"Now let's get this Confirmation started," Coach says. "Each night we have students of the Minor holidays present to us and the members of the Holiday Council their plans for the future of their holidays. This is the chance to see the vision that our future leaders have. The first up this year are two presenters who know each other well. They are the brother and sister team of Daylight Savings Time! Now let's welcome to the stage Spring!"

I clap loud and hard. I join in Columbus with whistles as Spring makes her way to the stage. I sure hope she got those slides finished.

"Ladies and gentlemen of the Council, distinguished guests, and my fellow students," Spring begins. She's so poised. I'm amazed at how well she looks considering that I know for a fact that she didn't sleep at all last night. Or really any in the past week.

"I will try to make it through my presentation quickly. That way, my brother will still be awake to make his." This gets a big laugh from the crowd. I can just picture Fall backstage right now, asleep. I shake my head because I know he will wake up right before he goes out, nail his presentation and then head right back to sleep.

Spring is a natural orator. She speaks with ease, smiling the whole time and making eye contact with the crowd. She reminds everyone of the basics of Daylight Savings time, known as DST. The fact that it was developed by a New Zealand scientist and not Ben Franklin, as everyone seems to think. She moves to the beginnings of the holiday in Germany and other parts of the world before making its way to the US and becoming law in 1966.

I feel a swell of pride to see her up there. To realize how far her holiday has come in such a short amount of time. With Spring in charge, DST will be a Major in no time.

Then comes the famous slides. Spring goes through a range of people and their reactions to DST. From the farmer who loves it because it gives him more daylight to work in the fields to the mom who has walked through a dangerous area after work and also appreciates the safety of the light. We all laugh at the testimonial of a retired grandfather who loves springing forward "because he gets more time on the golf course."

Spring concludes her presentation emphasizing that DST gives us more light which means more happiness. Whether that happiness is work, safety, or fun, it is all worth it even if you have to lose an hour of sleep. When she steps down, my row stands in ovation for her. Even though the tradition is that all students clap at the end of each presentation, my row is LOUD. I hope I'm half as good as Spring come Friday.

Fall moves through his presentation as smoothly as I knew he would. Using his humor and relaxed nature, he wows everyone. When he's finished, the Council is dismissed to make their decisions. They take hardly any time (a good sign) before they return to the stage.

Fairy takes the podium wearing a big smile as she announces that both Spring and Fall will be confirmed and returning to Holiday High next year. Fall erupts in celebration while Spring collapses in her seat looking like she's the one that will be falling asleep. While I'm so happy for both of them, I still notice the rock in my stomach. One night is done and I'm one step closer to my own presentation.

CHAPTER TWENTY-NINE

That night it's a celebration in my room. Spring is on top of the world as we girls gather to congratulate her. The only person who's happier is Shadow now that she's "free from the shackles of that dreadful uniform." I sit on my bed and smile as Columbus, April, and Spring dance around singing karaoke.

I'm trying hard to stay in this moment, to savor and enjoy it. I want to bottle up this feeling and keep it with me forever. I long to stay here. I can't believe I'm thinking that, but it's true. I love these girls. I love my room. I LOVE the food here. And Patrick. Do I love Patrick? Am I even old enough to know what love really is? All I do know is that this is the place I want to be.

And then it is Friday. I'm in a deep sleep. I'm stuck in a dream where I'm running through the halls of the schools. Everywhere I turn in the dream I see more and more ice. It's covering everywhere I look. I can't enter any of the rooms because the handles are too cold. I can't sit on any of the furniture because it solid ice. I keep chasing a bright light that will appear down one hall but when I reach the spot it has moved and is now somewhere else. It moves and moves and I just run.

I jerk awake and I'm freezing. I'm drenched in a cold sweat, all my pillows are cold. I sit up and catch my breath and try to shake the cold. At first, I'm shivering so much that I didn't even realize that today is THE day. My alarm blares alive scaring me to death and I tackle it into silence. I'm sitting on the floor when it hits. It's Friday. It's 7 A.M. and my parents will be here in 12 hours. My stomach is a pancake flipping over and over as I think about them watching me in the Confirmation. Watching me fail in the Confirmation.

I drag myself up and start my day. Columbus made me promise that I would spend the morning of the Confirmation exercising the body before the mind. I pull on my official HH sweats and head to the gym. Before I even get to the door I hear the grunting. Columbus is famous now for the extreme noise that she produces while working out. I stop for a second just to make sure that I really want to enter this insanity.

When I enter I immediately want to turn around. Columbus is in the middle of the gym doing lunges down the center of the court while holding and lifting two kettlebells. A loud grunt escapes with every lunge. She finally gets to the end of the court and turns around to finally notice me. "ARBOR!" she screams and I jump. "Start stretching and when I get back to you we will begin. Today is your Confirmation Day!" I start to plan to my escape.

"There is no Escape!" Columbus grunts at me. "Start stretching!" She starts to make her way back down the court and I start to stretch. At this point, fear is winning me over more than anything. Columbus reaches the other side of the court and I'm as stretched as I'm going to be.

My friend is drenched in sweat and not smelling the best. "How long have you been here?" I ask her.

"The early bird kills the worm, Arbor!" She answers at me, jumping up and down. "I've been here since 6 a.m."

"You're crazy," I answer back.

"And you had better be ready," she says. "By the time we're

done, you're going to be so pumped that nothing is going to scare you." What have I gotten myself into?

Columbus spends the next hour putting me through the rigors of what she deems her "mild workout." We start with jump ropes. Two minutes on with 30 seconds off for 10 minutes. We then spend the next 20 minutes running up and down the bleachers at the side of the gym. I spend the next 5 minutes begging for my life.

"Do you think you can beg the Holiday Council?" she yells at me. I'm amazed that she has already been here for an hour before me and is still running rings around me. Where does this girl get this energy?

We finally stop for a minute and I think it's over, but really the moment is used for Columbus to pour some wicked nasty drink down my throat.

"What is in that?" I spew at her with green liquid pouring down my front. "You don't want to know. Now let's move!" She says, pushing me toward the mats that are sitting on the side of the gym floor. Ten sit-ups. Ten pushups. Ten jumping jacks. Over and over for ten minutes.

At this point facing the Council and the Confirmation is a welcomed event. When Columbus finally calls break, I collapse. I'm exhausted in a good way. I feel the burn going through my body. I feel strong.

My coach disappears into a side room. When she returns she's dragging a body! I do a double and realized that it's just the upper torso of a man attached to a base. She sets it up and then she moves out of the way and I scream.

"YES!" I yell. "Bring it on!" Columbus has put Frost's face on the head of the body. It's perfect. He is looking down at me with that smirk of his. I feel the aggression building up in me and I wait for my cue.

"Are you ready Arbor?" I am asked.

"Ready," I say.

"Then... ATTACK!"

I dive in will all my force. I start punching and kicking and scratching. Columbus yells me on and I go and go until I'm totally spent. I collapse and know it's me who is drenched in sweat. Columbus gives the Frost dummy one giant kick knocking it over and then pulls me up onto my feet.

"That was awesome," she says, embracing me in a nasty sweat-filled hug.

"Yeah, it was," I reply. "But I'm starving."

"Good news," Columbus says. "I have more green power juice left!"

Chapter Thirty

That afternoon is spent going over my presentation in my mind. Unlike Spring who wanted to present to live people in the weeks leading up to the Confirmation, I just want to zone out by myself and play my speech like a movie in my mind. Before long I'm dressed and heading downstairs. As I make my way around the bend of my hall and head downstairs I see my parents have just arrived.

"Arbor!" My mom squeals as soon as she spots me. I'm barely to the bottom of the steps when she embraces and squeezes the life out of me. I take it back. Spring's hugs are nothing compared to how tight my real mom can compress me.

"That's enough, Hun," my father interjects. "Keep her alive so I can hug her, too." My mom lets go and my dad embraces me the opposite; soft and gentle. "Lots of mushy, mushy stuff," he whispers.

"So much mushy stuff," I whisper back.

We heard the announcement for the students to line up and our reunion is cut too short. My parents go into the auditorium and I line up with the rest of the students. I arrive late so I'm stuck at the end. I think I'm the last one to get there but I'm not. Lining up right behind is Valentine. "Good luck tonight, Arbor," she says.

I don't even turn around. "Thank you, Valentine," I retort back.

"No really, Good luck," She continues on. "You're going to need it." I continue to ignore and wait to enter. I feel a short jerk on my shoulder and I get twisted around until I'm facing eye-to-eye with Valentine.

"Don't ignore me when I'm speaking to you," she says, putting her face right up in mine. "I've put up with you and your self-righteous attitude all year and I want you to look me in the eye when I tell you that no matter what you do in there, it's not going to matter. You can give the greatest presentation that this school has ever seen, and it will do you no good. None. At. All." By the time she's finished, she's heaving her chest up and down, breathing hard.

"And why is that?" I asked her out of spite. "How do you know so much, Valentine? How is it that you're so sure that no matter what I do in there I don't stand a chance? Who do you even think you are?" I don't back down. I stand just as close to her and look her dead in the eye. Just like she wanted.

We stand there face to face. Neither of us saying anything. "I know everything," says Valentine, breaking the standoff. "Again, good luck, Arbor. Besides, does anyone really care about trees?" With that, she bumps me on the shoulder and walks by. Leaving me standing alone.

I take a deep breath and follow her in. Each time I've entered this room each of the previous nights I've admired the pomp and circumstance of the event. Not tonight.

Tonight it is different. It's like a tomb to me. Cold. I nod at my parents who are sitting in the third row, Mom waving like crazy. Their confidence in me is encouraging. I hope I can channel that when presenting. A jolt of life.

Each night this week has gone smoothly. The way that it

should and I try to tell myself that it will be the same tonight. All Minors have been confirmed quickly and with enthusiasm. "It will be so tonight," I repeat to myself over and over.

I head backstage and join J.J. in the green room. She's the other presenter tonight. Since her holiday isn't an official American holiday she doesn't have to worry about the Confirmation of Chinese New Year. She's the exact opposite of me. She's sitting comfortably, drinking a bubble tea and smiling when I enter.

"Arbor!" She greets me. "Can you believe the school year is almost over? Tomorrow we go home!" I can't help but smile. I've loved getting to be around J.J. all year and this may be the last time we may see each other.

"Yes J.J., you're right!" I say back to her. "This year has gone by super-fast. Are you ready to go back to Taiwan?"

"Oh, yes!" She answers. "I miss my family, my friends, and I really miss the food!" I laugh with her. I'm sure that nothing that Muffin has created can compare to the food of her homeland.

"I wish you the very best," I say. "Tonight and forever." J.J. rewards my words with the biggest smile in the world.

"It's time J.J.," Coach Bunyan says and pokes in his head. "I wish the both of you the best of luck tonight." J.J. gives me a quick hug and makes her way onto the stage. I hear a big ovation for her. I sit down, take out my notes and try to focus.

I hear plenty of laughs and applause coming from the audience during J.J.'s presentation and it puts me at ease. It sounds like everyone is in a good mood and really responsive tonight. That can only work in my favor.

I hear J.J. close her speech and the announcement of a 10-minute break. Ten minutes until I go. I have a funny feeling in my body. A mix of excitement and dread. But also a powerful adrenaline now that the moment is so close. I stand up and start to do some of the stretches that Columbus showed me that are supposed to "channel your inner spark."

"You getting ready to take the field?" I snap up out of my

stretch to see Patrick poking his head into the green room. Thank goodness my face is already flushed from the movement so that he can't notice how touched I am that he's here right now.

"Well, you know me," I say, blowing my hair out my face. "I was trained by the best coach there is." We both laugh since Columbus spent all day telling everyone how she "worked the fear" out of me.

"Listen," Patrick says. His face wearing that serious look of his. "You are going to do amazing. You have so much support out there. Your parents, your friends. You have me." He steps closer to me and takes my hands. "I wish I had something clever or motivational to tell you that will make you totally relax."

But actually I'm more relaxed now than I've been all week. Just in this calm moment before the storm hits. I wish myself to stay still in this moment and capture it. Like an old photo that I will keep for years to come. One that I will show my children and their children. Yes, at this moment I'm calm and relaxed. I tell Patrick so.

"That's good," he says, laughing. "I'd hate to think that my coming back would make you worse. Don't worry about anyone else. Block out Valentine. Block out Frost. Present from the heart."

With those words he has to leave as Coach tells me it's one minute. Patrick takes one last long look in my eyes and lets my hands go. Then I'm alone. I hear Coach addressing the crowd, telling them that we're down to our very last presenter of the week. He announces my name, I hear the applause, and I step through the curtain.

CHAPTER THIRTY-ONE

The lights are very bright. That's my first thought when I make my way onto the stage. They take me aback and I stumble a bit. I feel some strong arms steady me and I look up to see Mr. Groundhog, Shadow's dad, holding me up.

"Now, now, Arbor," he speaks to me softly. "My little Shadow has told me how amazing you are so we can't have you stumble right out of the gate."

I look at him with such relief and gratitude. I feel like I did when I was a kid and realized that I didn't have to get a shot at the doctor. "Thank you so much," I say.

"You are most welcome. Remember that you have friends here on this stage."

With that, he guides me the rest of the way to the podium. I ignore Frost completely as I pass him. I steal a quick glance at Fairy and she gives me a short nod that I take as, "We have trained for this. You will do a wonderful job and I'm so proud of you." She may not have been saying all that but that's what I chose to think.

I really underestimated how quiet this place can be when someone is about to speak. I can barely make out anyone in the audience. I can see my parents seated in the parents section. My mom is grinning from ear to ear. My dad is all business. I choke back some fear as I know the future of our holiday could be riding on what I'm about to say. I close my eyes and I begin to speak.

I jump right into the history of my holiday and how it's anything but "minor" in my world. The name J. Sterling Morton is a household name where I grew up. But most people don't even know the name of the man who started Arbor Day.

I continue on growing more relaxed and confident as I go. Fairy was right. Spring was right. Patrick was right. I can do this. I'm prepared and my energy level is strong. I must remember to thank Columbus for her green power juice.

Everyone within earshot of me now knows that on that first Arbor Day, April 10, 1872, one million trees were planted and many of them are still standing today. I joke about how I've longed to get that date tattooed on me, but my mother has made it her sworn mission in life to prevent that. I'm relieved when everyone laughs, and I smile big when I hear Shadow boo my mom's decision.

I show a slide picturing Teddy Roosevelt proclaiming "Arbor Day" to all the schoolchildren of the US on April 15th, 1907. Another date I explain that I want to get tattooed also. Shadow is heard letting out a "Whoop! Whoop!" from the back.

"By 1920," I continue, "All the states in the union had declared an 'Arbor Day." This goes to show that my holiday isn't just confined to states that have a large population of trees. Or states that are large. It's for every single state that we have. All 50." I hit everyone with a barrage of rapid-fire 39 slides depicting the 39 other countries that celebrate Arbor Day. I surprised everyone with a slide showing J.J. and her family planting a tree on Taiwan's March 12th Arbor Day.

After this rapid-fire section of my presentation, I slow it down and show 3 slides of students from my classes that I taught back home. Each slide is followed by a video of the student talking about their love and respect for trees. At this point, I'm in my own world enjoying my students and I forget all about the Council, my parents, and the others in the room.

I move on to the statistics portion of my presentation. I show them the decline of trees in different parts of the United States and the effects that could have over the next 20 years. I compared them to areas where Arbor Day is strong and represented.

My blood starts pumping and I'm getting excited. I'm on a roll as I lay out a 20-year plan on how to increase the influence of my holiday and the impact it can make in the areas with a shortage of growth. I plead with everyone to plant a tree. It doesn't matter that I feel like a cheesy, late-night infomercial. This is my passion. I want to be the catalyst to carry the charge of my holiday. It suddenly hits me what this whole year was about.

No longer can I sit back and expect my parents to do everything. I can't be satisfied with simply teaching my little classes and staying safe in my own selfish world. Being the leader of a holiday means giving of yourself. Making sure that the holiday is strong even at personal sacrifice to themselves.

Tears swell up as I explain that passion. I turn to address the Council and tell them that I get it. I understand. Holiday High is the place for me. I want this burden. I want this role. I was called to this. Arbor Day is my holiday and with their help and the help of all the staff here I can take MY holiday to heights it has never seen.

"But I can't do it alone," I say, pausing to gather my thoughts and slow my beating heart. "If I've learned anything from being here this year it is that the Holidays are not supposed to be disjointed."

"We shouldn't be expected to be out there on our own fighting our cause by ourselves." I continue, "We are stronger when we're together. We are stronger together. Each and every one can and should work together." I take a deep breath, let it out and I head into my conclusion.

"What I'm proposing today is a deliberate and calculated effort for the holidays to work together. An organized effort put forth by the Council in which they pair up holidays each year. Within that year the holidays work to encourage, support, and find ways to build off each other. All of which will do nothing but build their counterparts' holidays."

"This is even more important that you pair up the Majors with the Minors," I go on. "Imagine what impact Christmas could have on Veterans Day? Imagine the craziness that Halloween and Mardi Gras can cook up." I expect and get a laugh to that one and I use it to slow myself down.

Now is the time to take it home. "It will start with me," I say. "I propose that today I partner up hope with a holiday that I feel can motivate me to become the better leader that I want to be. I want to pair with this holiday because I want to be pushed. I want to take Arbor Day and bring it to a new level. "

"The holiday I wish to pair with is Valentine's Day." The room goes silent then. I see everyone strain to see Valentine's reaction. But despite the anger that I expected, I see something that looks like....well it looks like...intrigue? Could it be that Valentine isn't rejecting this idea right from the start like I figured she would?

"If you know anything about Valentine," I say, pointing to my schoolmate, "She's dedicated, hard-driven, and focused. All things I need to be. Imagine a world where Valentine's Day was not only about the love you show your boyfriend, your girlfriend, or your spouse, but it becomes something so much more. It begins with something where you show love to your planet. To nature. And if I'm being selfish, you show some love to trees."

I sneak a look at my parents and see now that my Dad is the one smiling ear to ear. My mom is crying softly and looking at me with a proud look I've never seen before.

I conclude my speech, by recapping the history of my holiday, the need for more trees, and my plan to pair up the holidays. I step down. I feel a smack of applause and the crowd shows their support. I see my friends jumping up and down celebrating and I notice Spring is already making her way to the front. I take a bow and step down off the stage. My parents come forth to embrace me but are blindsided out of the way by Spring tackling me down.

"That was AMAZING!" she screams into my face. "And those slides! They were awesome." We both laugh and cry as she helps me up. My parents hug and kiss me.

"So much mushy stuff!" my dad exclaims. "The biggest amount of mushy stuff ever!"

"I love you, too, Dad."

The rest of my group are there soon. We clap high fives and exchange hugs. "I'm taking you to get those tattoos right away," Shadow says once we're out of earshot of my mom. I'm exhausted but happy. Drained of energy but filled with joy. Now the waiting begins.

CHAPTER THIRTY-TWO

The waiting continues. After the excitement of my presentation, we all settle down and wait for the Council to come back out. We wait and wait some more. Ten minutes has the been most they have taken for any Confirmation this week so when that comes and goes I start to feel some sweat forming underneath my uniform. When twenty minutes have passed I see everyone else start to fidget and get nervous as well.

"I'm sure they are just discussing how to wrap things up," Patrick says to me, squeezing my hand. After thirty minutes of waiting Coach makes his way back to stage.

"The Council has asked me to invite you all to go ahead into the dining hall to enjoy the refreshments," he says. "We will make an announcement when a decision has been made."

Everyone not connected to me starts to move towards the exits. My mom and dad head up to the stage to talk to Coach. I watch him explain and I can tell that he doesn't know anything.

"Well, sitting here isn't going to help anything," Spring says, jumping up. She jerks me up and starts pushing me towards the doors. "Everyone, let's move," she calls back.

I'm a zombie. At least that's my state as we shuffle down the hallway. We join the line with everyone else to go into the dining hall. My head starts to hurt. I feel like all the strength and adrenaline that was coursing through has just left. Fast. My stomach starts to cramp and I feel nauseous. "Excuse me, guys," I say, and start to head to the bathroom. I wave off Spring as she starts to follow. I just need to be alone.

But I'm not alone. I close the door behind me and lean on it to catch my breath and calm my swirling head. I faintly register the sound of rushing water but I'm so wrapped up I don't fully comprehend.

"Feeling a little nervous?" A voice breaks through bringing me slowly back around. I open my hands slightly and shake my head. Great this will be awkward.

"Hello, Valentine," I say. My eyes close again and I wish myself away. Or at least back to the moment with Patrick before my presentation.

"So," she says. "We are supposed to be partners now?" I slowly clench my fists open and shut trying to bring some feeling back to my hands.

"I'm sorry, Valentine," I begin. "I was just stating an idea—."

"No. Let me finish," she says, cutting me off. I slowly brace myself.

"It really isn't a bad idea," Valentine says to me. Now that snaps me back into focus.

"Excuse me?" I ask.

"Don't get me wrong," She continues. "I don't like you. I don't think you have what it takes to lead a holiday. But..." she pauses. But what? I think.

"What you said had merit. I would love my holiday to become more than just flowers and hearts and those nasty conversation hearts." I chuckle.

"My mom loves those things," I say. "We have to hide them from her, we call them her crack."

"I hate them," She answers back to me and I stop my chuckle.

"Listen. If for some reason you're confirmed...." she says looking me in the eye. "...If for some reason you're here next year, we can try this partner thing you're talking about. Lord knows you need more of me in you." With that, she pushes past me and is gone.

I wash up and join my friends at our table. My mom and dad have joined us and I sit between them. They are both encouraging and I try to relax. If this is my last time sitting here then I might as well enjoy it. I join in with the others putting straws in Fall's hair as he sleeps. I nibble on my cheesecake muffin and try to calm myself down. Columbus is in the middle of explaining to my Mom the green power juice recipe when Coach's voice comes over the speaker announcing that a decision has been made. It has been over an hour.

As we're filing back in I notice that Fairy and the rest of the Holiday Council are already on stage. I try to make eye contact with her but she's too busy speaking with Santa. I settle into my seat. Sandwiched in between Patrick and Spring I feel as safe as I can possibly feel.

Fairy makes her way to the podium. As soon as I see her face I know something isn't good. "Ladies and gentlemen," she begins, "I apologize for the delay but our young Arbor here has given us some real things to ponder." I take in a breath and try to focus on small even breathes. I suddenly wish that I had joined Shadow on her morning yoga sessions. "Ms. Day's presentation was precise, inspirational, and outstanding." " She says the last word with a big smile and I'm hoping that I had misread her earlier.

"With that said it's my pleasure to announce that Arbor Day has been confirmed and will be returning to Holiday High next year." Spring is the first one out of her seat. She's screaming, jumping, and jerking me up all at the same time. Flag stands on the seat in front of me arms raised high in victory. All my friends are congratulating me. My parents join us and I'm stunned. It's done. Finally. I did it. But Fairy isn't done. "Excuse me, everybody," she speaks into the microphone. She makes the universal sign for sitting down and while it takes a bit, she gets the attention of the room again.

"I'm so pleased that Arbor has been confirmed and it's well deserved," she says with her face taking that serious tone I saw earlier. "But while she's confirmed it is done not without some changes." With this she pauses, obviously pained with what she's about to say. We are all quiet.

"I believe in Arbor Day," Fairy speaks. "Not only the holiday but the person. I've spent the best part of this year as her mentor and while it wasn't always pretty, and she can be a very stubborn, fiercely independent young lady. But she's the type of leader that we must have here at Holiday High and that we must have leader our holidays into the future." She stops and looks directly at the students of the school.

"It's that belief in her and my belief in her future that I've agreed to step down as Principal of Holiday High in order for her Confirmation to go through. Vice Principal Frost is taking my place as Principal in the next school year." With that, the whole world moves into slow motion.

The majority of students are up in their seats yelling at the stage. I slowly see Santa rushing onto the stage and arguing with Father Christmas. Fairy is trying to calm the scene down. I hear nothing and I'm viewing everything in molasses. I see the pain and outrage of the students, and the bewilderment of the faculty.

I feel the tears slowly coming down my cheeks as I scan the stage trying to make sense of what was just said. I'm desperate to talk to Fairy, to tell her to not do this, to tell her I'm not worth this. But I don't move. I don't look at Fairy. Instead, my eyes lock onto the one person who staring directly at me. Frost.

Chapter Thirty-Three

The next morning I find myself drained. What a long night. Once all of the students settled down Fairy promised that she personally write each and every one of us a letter this summer explaining her actions and decisions.

Once I said goodbye to my parents I collapsed into my bed and didn't move for hours. I woke up in the middle of the night still in my uniform and I realized that I still haven't packed to go home. While I'm excited to be with my parents and teach my classes again I finally realize that now that I can be at home in two places. Something I never thought possible when I first arrived here.

So here I stand facing the same eight steps that I faced months ago. The irony isn't lost on me that when I arrived I could barely move my way up the steps and now I can barely move myself down the stairs where my parents await.

Since we're leaving so early no one else is awake. Part of me is fine with this. I wrote notes for all my girls and slid them under their doors. Sandman promised me that he deliver my other notes to the sleeping boys of our group. "I will take extra care of the note for young Patrick," he says, laughing and running away.

Step one: I start down the stairs with a heavy heart. Fairy will not be here next year. I'm still shocked by her announcement and the ramifications that it will have next year.

Step two: Frost is in charge. Frost is the principal. No longer will we have Fairy to control his emotions, his will. It will all start and end with him.

Step three is for Spring. *Steps four and five* for Columbus and Shadow. I settle for a moment on step 5. I find myself wondering if I will see Patrick this summer. He has promised letters, emails, postcards, carrier pigeons, and smoke signals. He is getting his wish to return to Ireland for the summer and I'm so proud of him. His father has even permitted a cooking course while he's there.

Step 6: Valentine. While there has been no official announcement from the Council in regard to my Holiday Partner Program, or HPP as everyone is calling it, Valentine's mother made the effort to speak to my parents about her support for the program and her desire for the two of us to gather this summer.

Step 7: I'm going to miss the food. No lie. Muffin is the man.

Finally, step 8 is here. When I arrived I stated that I hated this place. That I hated everything about it and the establishment it represents. But now that a year is gone and I've survived, even thrived, those emotions are gone. I take this final step not as the bitter, shy, resentful girl that arrived. I leave emboldened. I leave smarter.

I leave as the future leader of my holiday. It starts with this last step. I can't believe it.

Made in the USA
Middletown, DE
02 January 2024

47101690R00135